Modi @ Success India

Modi @ Success India

(101 Inspiring Stories from the life of Prime Minister Narendra Modi)

Renu Saini

Published by
PRABHAT PAPERBACKS
4/19 Asaf Ali Road,
New Delhi-110 002 (INDIA)
e-mail: prabhatbooks@gmail.com

ISBN 978-93-5266-980-6
MODI @ SUCCESS INDIA
by Renu Saini

Translated by
Prof. Ram Bhagwan Singh & Dr. C.L. Khatri

Price
₹ 250.00 (Rupees Two Hundred Fifty only)

Printed at
R-Tech Offset Printers, Delhi

To the citizens
who are harbouring positive change
in India with Prime Minister
Narendra Modi's insight.

Author's Note

A good number of books have appeared about Modiji. His life since his childhood is unobscured to the public like an open book. Every now and then new books about him are being published and gaining appreciationfrom readers and critics. One wonders, what's there in Modi's personality which leaves its own and exclusive stamp on people and inspires them. Whichever strategy Modiji adopts, it becomes a centre of attraction both for the public and the opposition. If he has influenced the upper class with his policies, ability, efficiency and work culture, he has also appeared before the common man as his Prime Minister. Today an ordinary man not only can convey his words to a man of unique and exceptional personality like Narendra Modi with ease, he can also meet him. Perhaps this is also one of the secrets of his success that while meeting every person he can resonate his thoughts with him.

The personal life of Modiji has been one of fierce struggle. He has faced every challenge courageously. The gusts of storm and struggle have taught him never to give in to the worst of circumstances. The struggle has tried him and proved his mettle. Decisions on the home front, foreign tours and his vigorous speeches have mesmerized the whole world. Everybody is aware of these facts. So what's new in this book which will draw the reader's interestwith delight.

In this book, the progressive journey of Modiji right from his childhood till this day has been presented through stories. At times where the information or fact tends to become monotonous, there the stories make them interesting and palatable. From centuries stories have been the inseparable part of people's entertainment. When someone wants to learn something well, the medium of storiespresent fact or information most effectively. Knowledge and information imparted through stories linger on for centuries. With this idea this book has been written. If even a single story finds favour with the reader, then the effort of writing this book will be justified.

—Renu Saini

Content

Modij's Childhood

Two small kids, Som and Amit were playing in a house. The women of the house were busy looking after the kid's mother Hira Ba. The birth of a new child was expected, so there was much activity around. This was a house situated at Vadnagar in Gujarat which is famous for its cultural beauty. A number of legends are related to this city. It is believed that there lived two sisters named Tana and Riri in Vadnagar. The two sisters practised and perfected music. From the mellifluous voice of the two sisters even the wind changed its direction and cool air flowed all around.

Tansen is known to everybody. He was an ancient singer and musician. He is immensely famous for his musical compositions. He was one of the nine gems in the court of Mughal Emperor Akbar.

There is also a myth that when Tansen sang, the lampswere lit all by themselves. Similarly when he was singing Raag Deepak, his body started simmering with heat. Sick with heat in the body, Tansen set out in search of Malhar singers. Tana and Riri sang Malhar, only then Tansen's body heat was satiated. The Malhar of Tana and Riri gave a new life to Tansen at that time.

In such a place on 17th September, 1950 Narendra Modi

was born as the third child in the house of Damodardas and Hira Ba. There was great jubilation in the house. The two elder brothers of Narendra Modi were overjoyed at the arrival of a younger brother. Damodardas and Hira Ba had six children in all. Among them Narendra Modi was the third. After Narendra Modi, his sister Vasanti, then two younger brothers Prahalad and Pankaj were born. Thus, Narendra Modi spent his childhood playing with his elder and younger brothers and sister.

The six children along with their parents lived in a 40' x 12' house. Father Damodardas and mother Hira Ba were very much hospitable, cultured, disciplined and eager to serve. They also taught their children such things. The economic condition of the house was not good, so the children went to the government school at Vadanagar. One day seeing Som and Amrit preparing for school, Narendra told his mother, "Ba, I will also go to school with my brothers. Prepare me also to send me to school."

Noticing the desire of a small Narendra to go to a school Hira Ba said, "My child, you are too small. They will not admit you to school . When you grow up a little more, I will also get you admitted to school." Little Narendra half understood his mother's words and half did not. But without a doubt, as his brothers would return from school, he would surely turn over their books. At times out of curiosity taking a pencil in hand he would scribble something on the wall or stone. One day Damodardas found that Narendra taking a pencil in his small hands was drawing criss- cross lines on the wall outside. Seeing him engrossed in his fun, he kept looking on him attentively. He called in Hira Ba and showed her how Narendra was passionately engaged in drawing criss-cross lines on the wall. Hira Ba was astonished to see little Narendra's passion. She lifted him up and embraced him Damodardas also felt overwhelmed. He told Hira Ba, "This child of ours will be very intelligent. If only I could give him good education." Then his eyes got moist.

After growing up Narendra started going to the same government school at Vadnagar and had his primary education there. Thereafter he had his secondary education at B.N. High School.

□

Forms of Nadi in Sanskrit

One day the teacher was teaching Sanskrit in the class. Narendra was also reading his Sanskrit book. That day the teacher taught the students different forms of nadi. He also taught a lesson in Sanskrit. A student said, "Sir, it is not easy to memorize the different forms of dev and nadi. Please teach us the easy way to memorize them." Hearing it all students echoed, "Yes sir, sometimes the forms of dev or the form of nadi create confusion."

Hearing the words of students the teacher said, "The forms in Sanskrit are difficult to look at but if you look at them attentively, it is easy to know and remember then, Then, he addressed the class, "You people memorize them like this- karta ne, karma ko, karan se.... When you learn this kartha, Karma rhythmically like a poem, it will be easy to remember the other forms of Sanskrit." Thereafter he taught those forms in a simple way writing on the blackboard. Now several students had followed the forms of Sanskrit words.

As the closing bell rang, the teacher picked up his books and moved towards the other class. While leaving he told the students, "Boys, today I have very sincerely taught you the lesson and forms of Sanskrit. Tomorrow all of you will write in your notebooks the forms of nadi and submit it to the monitor, "All students agreed with the teacher. But Narendra was not one with it. He told the teacher, "Sir, earlier all students had difficulty in understanding the different forms of nadi. You have taught us all equally well. In this way even the class monitor is an ordinary student like us. How can he judge whether what we have written is right or wrong. For examining the copy only you are competent enough and not the monitor. The monitor is himself a student."

The teacher was impressed to hear the words of Narendra. He said, "All right, all of you will present the forms of nadi. I will myself examine the copies of all of you. Your objection is correct. Even the monitor is not fit enough to examine the forms of nadi.

Thus, next day the teacher himself examined the copies of all students of the class.

□

Generous Narendra

It was a hot summer. There was no wind at all. All old and young were huddled together in rooms to protect themselves from the scorching sun. During that time Narendra had been to the N.C.C. camp which hehad joined in the school. He found the activities of N.C.C. very attractive. In N.C.C. along with unity and discipline they were asked to help the needy. All students under N.C.C. would become self-sufficient and do most of their works themselves. Narendra would listen attentively to every instruction that was given in N.C.C. One day all cadets were taking a rest in the camp. Students were not allowed to go out of the compound. While the coach and school teacher Govardhanbhai Patel where moving round the compound, the coach saw that a cadet was on top of a pole. Seeing it the teacher and the coach got angry. They decided to punish him and coming out hurriedly moved towards him. Before they could say something to Narendra, they saw that Narendra was trying to extricate a struggling bird trapped in the pole. The bird was struggling for life and Narendra not caring about his own life was eager to save the bird. Seeing it both the coach and the teacher came forward to help him. With the help of the three the bird was safely rescued from the pole and kept at another place.

When Narendra got down the coach said, "My boy, you are a real N.C.C. cadet. You took it as your responsibility not only to save the life of human being but also of all creatures. I am very pleased to meet you. I have a feeling within me that one day you will illuminate the name of this country." The teacher also placing his hand on Narendra's head said with a smile, "Bravo my son, carry on like this."

Narendra materialized the words of the coach and the teacher and today as Prime Minister of the country he is always trying to push his country forward on the path of progress.

□

Dramatic Skill in Childhood

Those days Narendra was a student of class VIII. From his childhood he was conscious of social injustice and had his own way to express his resentment. Once with his friends he planned to stage a one-act play in the school on a social problem. He named his play "palu phool" (yellow flower). He worked hard for this drama. The Principal, teachers and students all were very eager to see this drama. The drama started. The story of the drama was ran like this. There was a Dalit family in a village. The Dalit mother had a son. Once he is taken ill. The Dalit mother made all possible effort for the treatment of her son. She knocked at the door of the doctor, she rushed to the quack and prayed on her knee to save her son. But the doctor and the quack refused to treat the woman's son because he was a Dalit. Disappointed from all ends she moved towards the temple. Even at the temple the priest stopped her at the stairs of the temple. The Dalit mother with tears in her eyes said to the priest that God belongs to all. Anybody can appeal to God. Human beings did not help me. My son's dying. If he is not given treatment and medicine, he will die. Now, I have hope only from God. Saying this the mother starts weeping. Seeing the mother weeping the priest's heart melts. He goes inside the statue of

God in the temple and picking up a flower from there gives it to the Dalit mother and says, "What you say is correct. God belongs to all. All have a right to his mercy. Take this yellow flower as a blessing from God."

The Dalit mother is very pleased to get the yellow flower as a blessing from God. With joyful tears goes to her sick son and finds that he is on the point of death. The yellow flower falls from her hand near the boy. Seeing this,the eyes of all people present filled with tears. They went on clapping for long. A few minutes later, the Principal called Narendra to him. He said, "My boy, you managed this play very skillfully. Your efforts were obvious from the play." Narendra smiled. Just then class teacher of Narendra's class came to the Principal and said, "Sir, the writer, director and actor of this play is this promising boy Narendra." At this the Principal kept looking at Narendra with wonder and cheered for him again and again.

□

Wise Narendra

Once, the Inter School Kabaddi competition was organized in the primary school at Vadnagar. The Kabaddi teams had two names. The first team was named "Kumar School No. 1" and the second team was named "Kumar School No.-2". The Kumar School No. 1 team had players from lower classes whereas "Kumar School No.-2 had big players. Narendra belonged to "Kumar School No.-1" team. Both the teams were to fight face to face. Everybody knew that having bigger and faster players very often the victory went to "Kumar School No-2". Seeing this a player of "Kumar School No. 1" told Narendra, "Narendra, you are very wise. You do something so that we may defeat "Kumar School No. 2". Now everybody said in one voice to Narendra, "Of course, you can do so." Hearing the zealous words of the students Narendra said, "If all of you feel like this, then I will surely try." When the match started with "Kumar School No. 2" he saw that the captain of No. 2 Umedi Ji was an expert in that game and he never lost any point. Narendra went on watching closely every single move of "Kumar School No. 2". Very wisely he noted down the strategy of their team. He noticed that the captain and players of No.-2 always moved from the right side towards the attack zone. Thereafter with his team he chalked out a strategy so that they could attack No. 2 and defeat that team. When the two teams were playing face to face, everybody believed that "Kumar School No.-1" would be defeated by a big margin. But as the "Kumar School No.-1" appeared on the ground they found that they were in a totally different form. They were aggressively fast and agile enough to defeat any team. The audience saw that match with bated breath. At last Narendra Modi's wisdom was crowned with success and his team defeated "Kumar school No. 2". Not only once, did he defeated "Kumar School No.-2" team but three times in a row.

At this the teacher Kanubhai told another teacher, "You saw how intelligence, organizational skill and agility defeats the strong. Today Narendra Modi defeated the strong through his wisdom."

Thereafter all friends embraced Narendra Modi and began admiring his intelligence and skill.

❑

The School Compound

Those days Narendra Modi was in High School. His school had no compound. The school administration had no money to erect the compound. Having no compound there was always fear of students' safety. Both the teachers and students were disturbed. The school's Silver Jubilee was near at hand. On the occasion of Silver Jubilee several programme where organized. The list of programes to be organized on the occasion was being prepared, just then Narendra had an idea in his mind. He told his friends, "We can plan a drama on the Silver Jubilee. From this drama whatever income we receive that can be utilized to construct the compound."

Hearing the words of Narendra another student said, "You have said a very good thing. That way money can be obtained for construction of the compound and then our school will be safe."

All students voiced their agreement.

In this way Narendra started making preparations for the drama along with his friends. All students were engaged in the work sincerely. With the help of his friends Narendra prepared a drama titled "Jogi Das Khuman". Along with Narendra, all students were laboriously preparing for the drama.

Narendra played the role of Maharaja of Bhawanagar in that drama. That item became the crowning glory of that Silver Jubilee. The staff of the school and students all admired the drama in the superlative.

A sizeable amount was collected from the drama. The school compound was constructed from that amount. After the compound was constructed the Principal of the school congratulated Narendra in the prayer meeting and told the students that "Every student should have the feeling in his heart as Narendra. All you students are the bright future of our country. Today as seeds are sown in your mind, so will you perform in the future. In that respect I see a bright future for Narendra." At the words of the Principal all students present at the prayer meeting gave a thunderous applause. All took a pledge before the Principal that they will also contribute their best for building the nation.

❑

Chalk Polish

The economic condition of Narendra's house was pitiablewhen was a school student. On several occasions the family had no money to get him a pair of shoes. In that his relatives used to help him. One day Narendra's maternal uncle came to his house. He saw that Narendra had no shoes to wear. Immediately he got him a pair of white canvas shoes. Narendra very much liked the shoes given by his maternal uncle. He took greatcare of his shoes. Since the shoes were white they became dirty quickly from use. Narendra had no money to buy polish from the market. He felt hurt to see his dirty shoes. He wanted to go to school wearing shining white shoes every day. But it was not possible as the financial condition of the family was not sufficient to indulge in such needs. When his eyes fell on the shining white shoes of his friends, he had a wish that his shoes should also be shining like them.

One day during lunch hour he was walking in the school premises. Suddenly he saw that small pieces of chalk were lying about the place. In order to clean the premise he picked up the small pieces of chalk to drop them in the dustbin. He saw that as he had picked up those pieces, the white dust had left its mark on his hands. Seeing that, an idea stuck his mind. He started collecting heaps of chalk pieces. When the school bell rang and students left for home, Narendra would enter the classroom and collect chalk pieces there. When enough chalk pieces were collected, Narendra ground them into powder and making a paste applied it to his shoes. When the chalk powder dried up it became white and Narendra was overjoyed to see that his shoes were shining white. In this way right from his childhood wise Narendra applied his mind to new things and sought solution to each problem.

Now, he too, attended his school wearing his shoes shining white with chalk polish.

❑

Baby Alligator

Narendra Modi loved discipline since his childhood. He never disobeyed his parents. He was very fond of bathing in the pond. One day he went to theSharmistha Sarovar with his friends. There he saw that a baby alligator was swimming happily. Narendra kept looking at that baby alligator with keen attention. The friend said, "Narendra, let's go swimming like this baby alligator." Narendra replied, "I find this baby alligator very cute. I will take it home." He took out that baby alligator from the pond and brought him home. Seeing the tiny alligator his mother said, "Narendra, why did you bring him in?" Narendra spoke innocently, "Ma, it looked very dear to me. When he was running hither and thither in water, I enjoyed it. Therefore I brought him with me. Now I will go on playing with him."

Hearing the innocent words of Narendra, the mother Hira Ba stroking his head said, "My boy, you did not do the right thing to bring in the baby alligator here. It is not a good thing to separate a child from his mother." At this Narendra said, "Ma, but he is totally safe in our house." Mother said, "My son, if somebody separates you from me and gives you all the ease and luxuries, will you feel as happy there as you feel with here me?"

Narendra was taken aback to hear the words of his mother. Worry lines immediately appeared on his face. He said, "Ma, how can I live away from my family! I will be no more away from you. What use are those luxuries when you are absent in them." Then Narendra looked at the baby alligator who was restlessly moving about. He understood that he was lookingfor his mother and family. Immediately he became conscious of his mistake and very affectionately picked up the baby alligator. After a while he put him back in the Sharmistha Sarovar wherethe alligator joined his family. Seeing it Narendra showed feeling of satisfaction, over his face. Today his mother Hira Ba gave him a good lesson in life.

❑

Unusual Iron

Ever since his childhood, Narendra co-operated with his parents in day-to-day work. Very often, he helped his mother Hira Ba in her kitchen work. When his mother would be cooking food, Narendra would clean the pots and the kitchen. Not only this, when his mother was sick, he cooked food, too. There was shortage of facilities in his house, still he fully enjoyed his childhood with brothers and sister. He knew how to live blissfully even in want. One day his brothers and sister were looking at their school uniforms. Their uniforms had too many creases. Showing his uniform to elder brother Narendra said, "Brother, the creases in the uniform let me down. Generally all students came in uniforms which were well pressed. We don't even have a press. In the situation how can we remove the creases from our clothes?"

Seeing it his sister said, "Brother Narendra you are very wise. As you shine your shoes without polish, similarly you should devise a way to remove creases from the clothes." Hearing the words of his sister the youngest brother said, "Yes brother, you can surely find out a way." Now, Narendra went on devising a means to press clothes without an iron press. At last, he made it. He took a brass lota (pot) and put in it burning coal and very cautiously plied it over the creases on clothes. As the lota was hot it worked like a press.

Seeing it all brothers and sister were overjoyed. They said, "Brother Narendra, you are unparalleled. You have a solution to each and every problem. You are very wise." Hearing the words of brothers and sister even the parents began admiring the wisdom of Narendra said, "Really seeing the intelligence of Narendra, it seems that with his intelligence he will change the country."

The words of parents came true. Today donning the seat of Prime Minister Narendra Modi is intelligently working to make the country on top of the world.

❑

Father's Inter-religious Friendship

Kesimpa is a village near Vadnagar. From there Abbasbhai Momin used to come to V.N. High School, Vadnagar for study. Momin's father was a peasant. Whenever he came to Ganj Bazar he used to stay at Narendra Modi's father's tea stall near the railway station in Vadnagar. There was good friendship betweenAbbasbhai Momin's father and Narendra Modi's father. When Abbasbhai was in class VII, his father died. Abbasbhai was interested in studies. He continued coming for the study. Damodardas Modi had developed intimacy with Abbasbhai. When Abbasbhai came to class X it took him considerable time to go to and come from his home. Seeing it Momin's uncle came to Damodardas and said, "Abbas has to spend much time in coming from home to Vadnagar and going back. It hampers his study. In such a situation I don't know how to make arrangement for his studies?"

Hearing it Damodardas spoke after thinking for a moment," You needn't worry for it. Abbas will stay in my house. There he will study with Narendra and his other brothers and sister. To me Abbas is as good as Narendra. You leave him to us. It will not hamper his study in any way. Now you go home fully assured and don't worry about Momin's study."

Thereafter Momin stayed in Damodardas's house for a year. During this period the entire family of Narendra sincerely helped him for a full year. Mominbhai would always say, "I have been able to get higher education only with the co-operation and blessings of Damodar uncle. He has presented a beautiful example of secularism and humanism. Had he not come in such a situation to help me, my future would have been uncertain. Now when I grow up I also will keep up burning the lamp of secularism.

In this way since his childhood Narendra saw in his house an environment of communal amity. Such an environment played a pivotal role in developing his personality.

❑

Narendra's Friends

In his school days Narendra had several friends. But he was closest with Jasud Khan Pathan. Jasud had studied with him from class one to class XI. Both would sit on the same bench in class. In Vadnagar, their localities were also nearby. They shared many things in life almost all matters in school and in life. Not only this, Narendra helped Jasud Khan in other matters alongwith studies. Both celebrated each other's festivals with full sincerity. Whereas Jasud Khan indulged himself during Deepawali and Holi in the colour of Narendra, Narendra was seen embracing Jasud Khan during Eid. Jasud Khan waited for Deepawali more eagerly than Narendra did. Similarly Narendra eagerly waited for Eid and going to Jasud's house enjoyed the sumptuous vermicelli sweet dish. Whenever somebody said something to Jasud Khan, Narendra always came forward to defend him. Enjoying the pain and pleasure of student life both of them grew up. Since school days Narendra was attracted towards saintly life. He very much liked Swami Vivekananda. Whenever he read Vivekananda, he found in himself a flow of hope and confidence. He often told Jasud Khan, I am more inspired by Swami Vivekananda and other guru's life than general life.

Hearing the words of Narendra Jasud Khan often

remarked jokingly, "Narendra, I feel that one day you will play an important role in transforming the country. Your thoughts distinguish you from general people. I have been watching your thoughts since childhood. If you play a role in transforming the country I will be more happy than you."

Hearing it Narendra said smilingly, "Arre, not only I, all of us together will transform the country and there will be a wave of ease and happiness in the country."

At his words Jasud Khan smiled and said, "Yes Narendra, sure. We'll surely do that."

❑

Mother's Medicine

Narendra Modi's mother Hira Ba had a social outlook. She was ever ready to help people around her in all possible ways. Hira Ba was not educated but she had good knowledge of local medicines. She enjoyed God's special grace so that the person who got medicine from her, was very soon cured. Hira Ba gave medicines to the sick free of cost. Besides, most of the people who came to her were poor. When Narendra grew up he noticed that his mother got up at 5 o'clock in the morning and started giving medicines to the people. One day he got up early. Seeing him get up so early mother Hira Ba said, " My child, there is still much time to go to school. You take a rest now. I will wake you up in time."

At this Narendra replied, "Ba, I know there is still much time to go to school. I have got up early today to help you. You get up so early every day and we children keep sleeping. I like to see you distributing medicine to people."

Hearing the words of Narendra Hira Ba stroked his head with affection. She said to her, "My son, I felt very happy to see your interest in my work. Come, you also sit here along with me." Hearing the words of mother Narendra promptly got up from bed. Happily he had a bath and getting ready in no time sat beside his Ba. Thereafter Hira Ba went on telling about local medicines and Narendra went on listening attentively. He was very happy to see mother giving medicines to people. One day he told her, "Ba, do you have magic in your hand, whoever comes here says that he was cured from your medicines?"

At this Ba would say smilingly, "My boy, I just do my work with an honest mind, the real work is done by God." From the words of his mother Narendra developed a tendency towards social work since his childhood.

❑

Helping the Flood Victims

Those days Narendra Modi was a student of class IX. Unfortunately during that time as a result of heavy rain a flood like situation developed in different parts of the country. Public life was disrupted completely. Several parts of the country were devastated. Several villages in Gujarat around Surat were ravaged as a result of flood in the Tapi river. People were devastated because of heavy loss to life and property. Everywhere there was the piteous cry of pain. When young Narendra Modi saw the suffering of the flood victims he was touched to the heart. But what could a boy of 14-15 years of age do in such a dire situation?

Narendra Modi was quick witted since his childhood. He always found a solution to each problem applying his intelligence. To solve the present problem too,he began to think hard. He remained in a meditative mood for a while and then suddenly flashes of enthusiasm showed on his sad face. In Gauri Kund of Vadnagar, a fair was held in the month of Sawan every year. A large number of people used to come to enjoy that fair. In the fair the stalls of food articles and other times were in great demand. Narendra's father gave him a rupee to go to the fair and buy things of his choice. With a rupee in hand Narendra collected all his friends. Having consultation with friends it was decided that collecting contribution from friends they would open a tea stall in the fair and the income obtained from it will be distributed among the flood victims. Narendra brought in the necessary pots and stove from home. In this way with the help of friends a tea stall was opened at the fair. When Narendra prepared tea with his friends for the first time, all of them tasted it. Friends said, "Wow Narendra, you are superb in everything. Tea made by you has a unique taste."

Thus, they made sufficient money from the tea stall in the fair. Seeing it Narendra and all his friends were elated. They distributed the money earned from the tea stall among the flood victims. The eyes of flood victims filled with tears and gratitude to see the co-operation from young children and several people profusely thanked and blessed them.

❑

Helping the Jawans

In 1962 the war between India and China was going on. At that time patriotic feelings were rising supreme in the Indian minds. The Indian soldiers were fighting tooth and nail to protect the country. At that time Indian forces were moving both ways in large numbers in the trains passing Mahesana railway line near Vadnagar. Indian forces would board the train with great enthusiasm and alertness and would vow to leave no stone unturned to defeat the enemy. Narendra Modi was then only twelve years of age. Even at that age he feltthat a great calamity had come upon the country and it was necessary to get united for all Indians to cope with the disaster. One day he saw some service oriented people from Vadnagar at the Mahesana railway station whowere going to help the jawans. Without waiting for a minute he took permission from his parents and joined the service oriented group. After that, with those people at the railway station he engaged himself in serving food packets and tea to thejawans passing that railway station. Day and night irrespective of time, forgetting his own hunger and thirst donning the mantle of patriotism and nationalism he applied himself to the service of the jawans. On several occasions the trains' would pass, carrying the jawans in the dead of night. In such a situation young Narendra would keep awake till very late. As soon as the signal of trains arrival would be green, he would very boldly stand up and warmly welcome the jawans and serve them food articles. He would also ask them how to drive away the enemy.

Seeing Narendra a boy of 12 years a jawan said, "My boy, if the feeling of patriotism motivates such boys like you, no enemy will dare to touch the border of our county." Hearing the words of the jawan Narendra Modi said excitedly, "I will cut off the hands of those enemies that tend towards our border. I'll kill them."

Hearing the revolutionary words of Narendra a jawan remarked among his fellows, "One day this boy will certainly glorify the name of our country."

The words of those jawans proved true and today that boy Narendra, donning the position of Prime Minister is working hard to carry forward his country to a new horizon of glory.

❑

A Skilled Swimmer

Narendra Modi was fond of swimming right from childhood. He had not had any training in swimming. Playing with the boys of the village he automatically learnt swimming. He used to go to Sharmistha Sarovar of Vadanagar. That pond was full of crocodiles, so people avoided swimming there. Every year on the second day of Ashad the local people with a dagger in hand would reach swimming to the stand in the middle of the pond and plant their flag there. Narendra Modi would also start from near the library ghat and go swimming to the stand in the middle of the water. The pond would be filled to the brim. It was very risky to go swimming and plant the flag. There was also the danger of crocodiles. Narendra Modi was never afraid of taking risk anytime. Once he jumped into the Sarovar with his friends Bachu and Mahendra. Other people of the area went on playing on drums and cymbals to ward off thecrocodiles so that swimmers might perform safely. Narendra Modi with his friends went up to the stand and exchanging the flag came back safely. Seeing it all, the people present there started clapping cheerfully and welcoming him said, “Narendra, your courage and enthusiasm is really praiseworthy. In this dangerous pond it was because of your courage and enthusiasm that your friends also jumped in the fray, otherwise today it was very difficult to hoist the flag there."

Hearing the words of the people Narendra's friend said, "What you say is correct. At one moment I was also afraid but in the pond itself Narendra through gestures encouraged me and advised me to follow him. It was his courage which emboldened me. Really, it is a great thing to have a friend like Narendra." Bachu also endorsed the view of Mahendra. Seeing it, Narendra said with a smile, "You people also co-operated with me. If we live united we can do every risky and difficult thing very easily." At Narendra's words all people nodded in affirmation.

❑

Attraction towards Saints

Once there was a marriage ceremony at the house of Narendra Modi's maternal uncle. The uncle came and invited all people very affectionately. He asked Narendra in particular to attend the function. The maternal uncle was very much impressed by the intelligence and sincerity of Narendra. He felt that if Narendra would be there, the children around him would get an opportunity to learn from him. Narendra also felt attached to maternal uncle. He said enthusiastically, "Mamaji, I will surely come."

Maternal uncle went back and engaged himself in preparation for the function. A few days before the marriage in Vadnagar there came a hermit. He had grown wheat on his palms and over the whole body. Only his face was open. Because of jawar sprouts on his hand and over the whole body, he could not even eat with his hands. The public would come to see him and go back saluting him. When Narendra saw the hermit he realized the mental state of the hermit as he had to face much difficulty in getting food. He took upon himself the responsibility to feed the hermit with joy and enthusiasm. The elderly people told Narendra, "You are still a boy. Let somebody else do that work." But Narendra did not agree. Not only this, for looking after the hermit he could not attend the marriage function at his maternal uncle's house though he was very enthusiastic to attend that marriage function. Right from his parents to his brother and sister all were astonished to see the sacrifice of Narendra.

Narendra's father Damodardas Modi told Hira Ba, "This son of ours is really of a different disposition. Such zeal and spirit of sacrifice in children is very rare to see."

Hira Ba said, "You are right. Besides zeal and spirit of sacrifice he also has the spirit of service."

In this way since his childhood Narendra Modi showed the stamp of his uniqueness on people with rare merit.

❑

Astrologer's Prediction

In 1963, when Narendra Modi was thirteen years of age, Vadnagar was the centre of saints and swamis. Every now and then there would come saints and sadhus from far off places. One day a renowned sadhu came to Vadnagar. It was believed that the words of that sadhu were the words of goddess Saraswati. Whatever he spoke proved true to the extent that nobody could even contradict his predictions. It was the tradition in that village that the sadhu had his meal at somebody's house. There was remarkable love among the inhabitants of Vadnagar. They all lived in harmony. That day the sadhu was to have his meal at Narendra Modi's house. The sadhu came on time for the meal. The inmates of the house welcomed him very affectionately. Special food was prepared for him. The sadhu had his meal with love. He noticed that all children were well disciplined. After taking his meal the sadhu demanded to see the horoscope of all the members of the house. At that time Hira Ba had the horoscopes of her eldest son Sombhai and Narendra Modi. She gave them to the sadhu. He first picked up the horoscope of Sombhai. He looked at it very closely for a long time. After reading the horoscope he said, "This child will have a simple life, but he is destined to go to jail."

After forecasting about elder brother he began to read the horoscope of Narendra Modi. At first glance, the sadhu's eyes were awestruck and kept extending his eye lids in astonishment. Seeing this Hira Ba asked a bit concerned, "What happened, maharaj? Is everything all right? Is there anything unwelcome?"

The sadhu asked, "No, whose horoscope is this?"

Hira Ba replied, "This is my third son Narendra's."

Hearing this the sadhu said smilingly, "Ma, this horoscope is immensely influential. His horoscope shows two-things one to become a hermit and another to join politics. But it is certain whichever way he goes, his reputation will spread far and wide. If he becomes a hermit, he will be as great as Shankaracharya and if he joins politics he will spread his wings like an emperor. His decisions taken in politics will prove miraculous and most effective for the whole country. From this boy's merit a new Bharat would come up which would astonish the world."

The prediction of that sadhu came true. Years later Sombhai had to go to jail for a day because he was President of the employee's union and had organized an agitation. The government promulgated section 144 against him. Sombhai broke it. The police sent him to jail. The life of Narendra Modi is before us to see how he, with his intelligence, wisdom, tact and decisions, has shaken the whole world.

❑

Diversity of Work

One day Narendra Modi was watching intently the school teacher teaching at the black board. After the teacher completed his lesson he asked the students, "Boys, I hope all of you have thoroughly understood the today's lesson. If any of you has any doubts, he can ask questions to clear his doubts."

At this Modiji raised his hand. Getting a sign from the teacher he stood up and said, "Sir, you could teach this lesson in another way. That would have been easier to students." After that Narendra explained his method to the teacher in his own way. That time the teacher stopped him and asked him to sit down. He said, "You are too small yet and infuriate me saying that I have taught the lesson in a difficult way."

After school hour Narendra came back home. Ma was doing domestic work. Narendra always lent a helping hand to his mother. Seeing her work, Narendra went to her and said, "Ma, you unnecessarily lengthen a work. Look, this can be done easily and in a better way." After that he helped his mother in cleaning the house so skillfully that the mother kept looking at him for a long time. Ma said, "My son, you are really quick witted. New thoughts and techniques crop up in your mind and prove very useful. Seeing your skill it seems to me that one day with your skill and thought and your working style you will transform the whole county."

Hearing the words of mother Narendra bundled up the washings and made his way towards the pond. He also applied new techniques in washing clothes, so when he would go to pond to wash clothes, people watched him how innovatively he was washing clothes.

The words of mother Hira Ben came true. Today Narendra Modiji as Prime Minister of the country is leading his country to new heights with his new strategy and skill.

❑

Narendra Joins RSS

When Narendra was a school student, Chandrakant Dave was the Hindi teacher in Bhagwatacharya High School and conducted the branch of RSS. At that time when Narendra Modi came to know that there was branch of RSS nearby, he started going there regularly. At RSS they taught in detail about moral values and Indian culture. In a short time there was a deep impact of Indian culture on Narendra. He became fully engrossed in patriotism and sociability. At Vadnagar, many workers of RSS visited regularly to work for it. Seeing Narendra's interest and intelligence, the elders of RSS were very impressed with him. Once a well-known worker of the state level, Shri Vakil came to the branch. At that time Narendra Modi was also present. He was very much impressed by the ideas of Shri Vakil. Vakil also saw new hopes for the future in young Narendra. Thereafter he introduced Narendra to important people of the RSS. Narendra met everybody easily and listened to their views. Most of the learned people had new plans and schemes to take the country forward. The country had gained freedom sometime back, so educated people were eager to push up the country towards development. One day a teacher told Narendra, "My boy, it is essential to bring in a new dawn in the country so that our country may be in the forefront in industrial revolution and may keep pace with other countries of the world. When most of the young people realize their responsibility, apply new thought and means for development, the country will develop and go forward. Now young people like you alone can develop the country with ability and intelligence."

Hearing the words of the teacher Narendra said, "Sir, I will do my utmost to develop my country." The teacher said, "Bravo my boy! If every young man has such thoughts as yours, there will be no cause for worry. When all young men and others make concerted efforts for the development of the country, there will be unity and harmony to make every life rich and beautiful.

❑

Bargain with the Shop Keeper

Among six brothers and a sister Narendra was the only child, who often worked with his mother. Hira Ba would always tell Narendra with love, "My boy, you too, like your other brothers and sister play and mind your studies. Why do you engage yourself in domestic chores right now?" At this, Narendra would reply, "Ma, undoubtedly I play and do my studies but at the same time it is the duty of children like us to take care of our parents. If we don't care for you, who will?"

At this Hira Ba would stare at him lovingly. One day Hira Ba was going to buy vegetables. Narendra saw herand came running and said, "Ma, Ma ! I'll also go with you."

Hira Ba knew that Narendra would not relent so she took him along. Hira Ba bought 2-3 vegetables. Narendra noticed that his mother bargainedevery time with the vegetable seller. At last Hira reached an old woman. She was selling bananas. Hira Ba asked the old woman about the rate of bananas and then asked her to lower the rate. Seeing it boy Narendra said, " Ma, why do you ask her to lower the rate? Mother is waiting for a buyer for so long. Why don't you buy? If you buy bananas at her rate, she will feel happy."

Hearing the words of Narendra Hira Ba bought bananas

as per old woman's rate. Afterwards she told Narendra, "Arre beta, these fruit and vegetable sellers always ask for more than the reasonable rate. In that case it is necessary to bargain with them."

At this Narendra said, "Ma, while buying costly items we don't bargain like this, then why bargain too much with poor sellers? Even if they charge ten or twenty paise more what difference does it make? It will not make much difference to us but the poor vegetable seller will surely get the reward of their hard labour."

Hearing it from a child,Hira Ba stood astonished. Stroking his head she said, "My son, one day you will surely become a great man."

Child Narendra proved the veracity of the words of his mother and becoming the Prime Minister of the country he is committed to taking the country on a new path.

❑

Passion for the Indian Army

Ever since his childhood,Narendra felt very proud and encouraged to see the army.There was an Army School near Jamnagar. Seeing many boys in that school uniform he also had a desire to join that school. One day he told his mother Hira Ba, "I very much want to join Sainik School. If I study in the army school I will join the army when I grow up and will serve the county."

Noticing the child's interest and curiosity mother Hira Ba stroked his head with love and said, " My son, I will talk to your father in the evening."

When Damodardas came, Hira Ba told him about the desire of Narendra. He said, "Where do we have so much money to send him there? To me all children are equal. It is my duty to give all the same kind of education. If we could not afford school fee it would be more difficult. I know that our Narendra is clever. Still I will make an attempt." Next day Damodardas Modi consulted a friend in this regard. Friend said, "Narendra is a promising boy. Take help from a relative and his future will be assured." Damodardas said, "The relative will help once but we will have to pay the fee every time. At present, the financial condition of the house is not so good."

Hearing everything the friend said, "Then I can't think of any other way out. I am also as poor as you. Had I some money, I would help you," Damodardas said, "No, no, I don't seek help from you. I am just talking so that we may find some way out and the child is satisfied." Even after trying his best Damodardas could not devise a way out. At last he said, "My heart says that whatever school Narendra joins, he will surely serve the country."

Years later the words of father were realized. Today Modiji as Prime Minister is a committed worker of the nation. ❑

M.A. Degree

Narendra Modi had come along with Vakil Saheb. There he was working sincerely as Sangh worker. Seeing Narendra work Vakil Saheb was very impressed by his sharp intelligence and dedicated working style. One day he told Narendra, "My son, God has given you such a sharp intellect. My opinion is that you should complete your studies. Now a days it is essential to be educated to go ahead in life." Thereafter Vakil Saheb himselfprocured for Narendra the necessary information regarding admission.Narendra Modi became post graduate by obtaining external M.A. Degree from Delhi University. He got guidance as an external student of M.A. from Prof. Praveen Seth. He guided him on new politics. Being a Sangh worker Narendra was very busy. So Prof. Praveen Seth helped him a lot. He provided him with notes on the subject. Narendra would take that file with him, read the contents and would come fully prepared. Gradually the examinations were drawing close. All students were preparing laboriously for the examination. Prof. Praveen Seth told Narendra, "Narendra, this is the time, you have to study diligently and pass the examination with good marks. If you pass with high marks, your future will be bright. One thing you must always remember that everything has a particular time. Now if you study diligently in your student life, you will do every work later in life as much diligently and you will be a success."

Narendra listened to the words of the professor attentively. He said, "Sir, I will remember your teachings all my life and will try my best to secure high marks in the examination. I will devote myself whole heartedly to studies." Later, Narendra appeared at the examination. When the result came all students including Narendra himself were astonished to see that despite being an external student for one year he had stood first above those doing the two years' course. In this way he stood first in the examination and imbibed in his mind the instruction of his professor. He went on doing everything sincerely and climbing the steps to success.

❑

The Reign of Gujarat

By the end of 1999 Atal Bihari Vajpayee was very pleased to see the clean image and working spirit of Narendra Modi. He had started including Narendra Modi in various important works. In 2001 the Musharraf-Vajpayee Summit Talk had heightened the stature of Narendra Modi. While facing the media Narendra spoke easily, politely and firmly. Narendra Modi the carrier of truth was doing his job with sincerity and single mindedness. On the morning of 2001 while Narendra Modi was doing his work devotedly, he got a message that Atal Bihari Vajpayee had called him immediately. That was a mild September morning. Getting the order from Atal Bihari Vajpayee, Narendra Modi approached him promptly and asked, "What's the matter? You have called me all on a sudden?" Seeing the facial expression of Narendra Modi, Vajpayee had a smile on his lips. He said, "Living in Delhi you have gained weight. I think by working hard now you should reduce your weight a little."

Hearing such strange words from him Narendra naturally showed astonishment on his face. He said, "I could not understand the meaning of your remark. You please tell me what hard work I should do?" Ataljee replied, "Go to Gujarat. There, contest an election. The public needs you there." Hearing such a thing abruptly Narendra could not make out anything of it. But he had to obey the captain. Narendra Modi came to Gujarat. There his astonishment was doubled. There he found that all the workers of BJP were very happy to learn that he was going to contest an election. After meeting Narendra Modi at Gandhinagar the Chief Minister Keshubhai Patel tendered his resignation on 4th October 2001. Narendra Modi was elected leader of BJP Legislative Party and 7th October, 2001 was recorded as a golden day in the annuals of Indian politics. That day Narendra Modi took oath of office as the 14th Chief Minister of Gujarat.

The stars of destiny were emboldened. Narendra Modi was given the crown as a reward for his dutifulness, honesty and industry. Thereafter he had a very busy routine. He girded up his loins to give Gujarat new shape and started working for it.

❑

Forest-Friend Welfare Scheme

Those days Narendra Modi was the Chief Minister of Gujarat. The work and efforts being undertaken by him were talked about everywhere. One day Narendra Modi was talking with some intellectuals and assessing the development in Gujarat. One of the teachers said, "Sir, the development of Gujarat is praise worthy, but even now we are not going ahead taking together some important people with us. If we include those people who are living in far off areas and are devoid of the basic facilities of life, certainly then the social and economic condition of the country will increase sharply."

The other people also endorsed the opinion of the teacher. The quick witted Narendra Modi said, "Today you have said a very important thing. The state government clearly believes that development should be all beneficiary,allinclusive and all of the country. To achieve this goal we will have to work for the welfare of the tribal people on priority basis. When the tribals' income will be double, all tribals will get education for their children, the tribal families will have their own homes, the quality of education will improve as per new era's standard, clean drinking water will be available to tribal families, there will be facility of pipe line. Irrigational facilities will be available for modern methods of farming; in tribal villages there will be basic facilities like- roads, bus stand, network of energy will be established, then everybody will develop." Thereafter "Forest-friend Welfare Scheme" was announced. From Forest-friend Welfare Scheme many tribal friends became partners in the development journey of Gujarat and today there has been a sea change in the life style and standard of living of the tribals there. Now the educated and active tribals are determined to make the whole country educated and conscious. As you enter Gujarat, the air and water themselves start narrating the story of their development.

❑

Save the Girl Child

Those days Narendra Modi was the Chief Minister of Gujarat. One day he was talking to people about the decreasing number of girl children in Gujarat. A large gathering stood before him. He said, "Today in Gujarat 840 girls are born against 1000 boys. Like the two wheels both men and women are equally required. In this respect the decreasing population of girls is a very big problem to think over."

At this a man from the crowd said, "Sir, the number of girls is decreasing because of female foeticide."

At this Modiji said, "The menace of female foeticide is not only in Gujarat, it has spread in every nook and cranny of Hindustan. We will have to find a solution to it. But I will begin at Gujarat. I feel very restless in the mind to hear about female foeticide. I am woefully pained." Another man from the gathering said, "Sir, female foeticide is happening mostly because of illiteracy. So it is necessary to educate the people." Modiji said, "What you say is totally wrong. From Umargaon to Ambaji there live tribal people. They are not educated like you and me. But the situation there is totally different. Even today the equation of boys and girls is equal in the families there.

Our brothers living in forests are not a party to this crime. We, educated and advanced people, kill the girl child in the womb itself. Yes, I agree with you that most people are not aware of what pain the foetus has to undergo while being killed." After that looking towards the people he said, "Do you know how much pain the female foetus undergoes at that time"? Hearing this from Modiji everybody lowered his head. Modiji said, "I have read. I want to tell you that today." The women from the gathering said, "We will surely hear, you please tell us." Many of the voices came from uneducated women.

Modi said, "From the fifteenth day the life of a child begins in the womb. That develops day by day. Each organ takes shape. As it develops its limbs begin to open, its eyes look around curiously in the womb.

During pregnancy when the foetus is killed, it tries to defend itself by crying in the mother's womb, but it is very sad that the new sprout fails to defend itself. In America in 1984 Dr. Bernard Netheson made a film on female foetus killing titled, "Silent Scream" which shows in detail how the foetus tries to defend itself from the killing instruments every moment and finally dies. Dr. Netheson's film shows how before the killing the female foetus changes its side in the mother's womb and plays comfortably. That time its heartbeat is 120 which is normal but as the instrument approaches to kill, its heartbeat rises to 200 and tries to hide itself in the mother's womb but the instrument kills that girl child quite mercilessly and writhing in pain the foetus dies before being born." Modi went on narrating it in his bold tone. When he spoke the last line, his own eyes where moist. Tears were obvious in most women's eyes.

Hearing Modiji several women came to Modiji and said, "We will all take a pledge to raise our voice against female foeticide and awaken the people to save the girl child."

It is a matter of surprise and happiness that after Modiji's emotional speech women became conscious and female foeticide was lowered in Gujarat.

❑

Woman as the Basis of Business

Once Narendra Modi was talking with rural men. Among them a man called Birju had a very narrow opinion about women. Modi said, "If we have to develop, we must work shoulder to shoulder with women."

At this Birju said, "Sir, women can handle only household. It is not for them to handle the country." Hearing it out of resentment Modi said, "What's this you're talking? If it seems to you like this, today I will tell you that the main basis of business in India is women. If there are no women the whole business world would come to a stop." Hearing it all men and women started looking at one another. Some men endorsed the view of Modiji.

Birju said, "Sir, women look after the kitchen only, then how is business dependent on them?"

Modiji said, "Birjuji the spice industry runs because of women. The women of Sabarkantha prepare spices with utmost care and spices manufactured by them are used in most of the homes. Similarly, from the co-operative society of south Gujarat the Lijjat papad industry came into being. There most of the workers are tribal women. That papad made by them is popular across the homes of India. If sisters make up their mind, they can do any difficult work in a trice.

In the same way Amul milk is on the lips of each and every child. Do you know that in the centre of the success of Amul there are our sisters sitting in villages? These sisters rear the animal stock and getting up early in the morning carrying the milk can on their heads go to the dairy; they keep the account. Because of the efficiency of these sisters the name of Amul is shining in Hindustan. Whether a big or a small unit if it is conducted by sisters, the benefit goes to the society manifold. Not only this, it has been being rumoured in the western countries that in India the position of women is very low. It is totally false. In the west women have been recognised now, whereas in our India long ago women like Gargi Maitreyee, Savitri Bai, Anandi Gopal and Leelawathi had registered the stamp of their work and skill. Not only this, in the freedom struggle the Rani of Jhansi, Durga Bhai, Jhalkari Bai and several other brave sisters' contribution cannot be forgotten. I condemn the view of each such person who has such a narrow view about women."

Hearing the words of Modiji, Birju lowered his head and realised his mistake.

❑

Unique Raksha Bandhan

The festival of Raksha Bandhan was being celebrated at the residence of Shri Narendra Modi, Chief Minister of Gujarat with great fervour. Sisters were standing ready with beautiful Rakhis to tie on the wrist of Narendra Modi. In a short while Narendra Modi appeared at the pandal. The Rakhi-tying session started. One after another sister came on to tie the Rakhi. Modiji was affectionately letting them tie the Rakhis. For him a festival was not meant for a single individual rather it was meant for the whole community, each and every Indian. When all sisters had finished Rakhi-tying, Modiji said, "Raksha Bandhan is not only the festival of love and safety, but also of social harmony and equality. Every positive aspect creates the hormone of zeal and makes people jovial and happy. The meaning of a festival in true sense is to live with love, peace and joy, to share joy with one and all. Come, you also tie Rakhi on the wrists of black commandoes engaged in security. These black commandoes living away from their families and sisters perform their duty. For them Rakhi and Deepavali mean- to ensure happiness and joy to our countrymen. This happiness and joy is possible to each citizen when our soldiers and commandoes sacrifice their all for the love of duty living away from the family. Therefore, today all you sisters let them feel that these commandoes are not away from their sisters, rather they are very close. Their family is not far off from them, they are with them every minute- in the form of each mother or sister." Hearing these words of Modiji, all sisters got up and began tying Rakhis on the wrists of the black commandoes. As the sisters raised their hands to tie Rakhis on their wrists, the stony hearts of commandoes were softened. When after tying Rakhis the sisters gave them blessings of long life, they told the sisters, "We also give the gift to our sisters that we will never tolerate any insult and affront on our country. We will sacrifice our lives, we will pluck out the eyes of those who cast an evil eye on our motherland."

The sisters treated the commandoes to sweets. That day both the sisters and commandoes were having a different kind of feeling of celebrating Raksha Bandhan in a different way.

❑

Togetherness with All

Once Shri Narendra Modi was talking to his staff. Suddenly he noticed that the sweeper was looking rather depressed. He called him near and asked, "What is the matter? Are you not well today?"

On being asked about his welfare by the Chief Minister of Gujarat, his lack-lustre face suddenly brightened. He said, "Sir, today my mother is not feeling well. I just remembered that, so I felt a little sad."

On the words of the young man Modiji patted on his back and said, "Don't worry, everything will be all right."

After his sweeping work later the young man left the place. After his departure Modiji told the officers in his duty, "We should behave politely with all our staff irrespective of their high or low position. This is the sign of Indian civilization, besides it shows politeness and a sense of co-operation."

At Modi's word an officer remarked, "Sir, what you say is absolutely correct."

Modi said, "The postman comes to our houses with the post. At times he comes with the post in the burning sun. In such a situation it is our duty to offer him cool water. Take it from me, drinking cool water the postman will feel refreshed and forget his tiredness. Every individual, every family, every society and every country can become powerful only if each individual of that country feels that he is someone special. You practise it right from today. You should know the person who cleans your office. You should regard the maid as important and equally treating the postman and the delivery boy give them a glass of water to drink. So that he may feel that realizing the complexity of their work at least there is someone who cares for them. From small works and their performers great things are achieved. We should not judge a person from his high or low work. Each work is important, so we should regard all works as important."

All officers present there endorsed those words. Modiji said, "When all people regarding themselves as important do their work responsibly, there will be no chaos, no dishonesty to see in the country. Only then the country will become better than heaven and dear to all. So, we should do our work like this so that there may be togetherness, co-operation and the feeling of love in all."

Just the next day an officer of the staff while talking to the other said, " I knew only yesterday that the daughter of the maid has secured 90% marks in class XII. I will help my best in getting her admitted to a good college."

Another officer said, "My driver's son has passed the C.A. examination." When Modiji heard the words of his officers, a smile spread over his face.

❑

S. P. i.e. Sarpanch Pati

Once Narendra Modi had gone to Haryana. There, a meeting was going on. People were being introduced at the time. Everybody was introducing himself/ herself. When nearly half of the people had introduced themselves a man stood in his seat. He told Narendra Modi, "Sir, I am S. P." Hearing S.P. in place of his name Narendra Modi asked, "All right my brother, granted that you are S.P. but in a meeting one should announce his name rather than his post. The real person is known from his name and work."

Hearing this remark that person said again, "Yes sir, what you are saying is correct. But I am known as S.P. whenever I go to a meeting, I address myself as S.P. by now everybody knows me by this very name."

People burst into laughter to hear the man's words. Seeing it Narendra Modi said, "May be, you are known as S.P. but I want to tell you that this meeting is not for SP rather it is being organized equally for all people present here. Before Narendra Modi could say something more, a man came near him and said something. From his words Narendra Modi felt very much surprised. Seeing Narendra Modi stupefied all people started looking at each other with surprise to know what had happened.

Dispelling the doubt and curiosity of people Narendra Modi said, "This gentleman is not Superintendent of Police, rather he is Sarpanch pati, meaning his wife is Sarpanch and he attends the meeting in place of her. This is very bad. Henceforth the woman Sarpanch herself will attend all meetings. Their husband will in no case attend the meeting for her." Hearing the words of Narendra Modi several women were overjoyed because they knew that willingly the husbands gave their wives permission to become Sarpanch but they themselves acted on their behalf and the woman Sarpanch got no opportunity to work. Thereafter, in all meetings women Sarpanch started attending meetings themselves and performing their duties.

❑

Modi's Simplicity

On 6 February, 2013 there was a massive gathering of students in the premises of Shree Ram College of Commerce. The crowd was eagerly waiting for Narendra Modi. In a chorus students were shouting "Modi.... Modi.... In a short while as Modiji stepped in, the jam-packed premises was agog with the cheers piercing the sky. It appeared that the black clouds echoed the voice to salute Narendra Modiji. Acknowledging the greetings of students Modiji started speaking. He was talking about the works and achievements of his government in Gujarat. Encouraging the students he said, "I am immensely pleased that the young people today are conscious of their future along with their studies and are inspired by modern ethics. The young are strong physically and mentally, they are full of energy and ever ready to accept the challenges of all sorts. Even gigantic obstacles cannot deter young men like you." Hearing the words of Modiji endorsing his views all students clapped in one voice. Modiji said, "I fully believe that after obtaining degree from this college you will engage yourselves in such activities that along with your progress, they will also take the society and the country to the path of development." Completing his speech as Modiji sat in his seat, the students surrounded him to ask their questions.

The Principal was overwhelmed with success of programme of inviting Modiji in his college. Just them someone out of curiosity asked the Principal, "There are some more other people who could be invited to be the Chief Guest here, some of them are even more reputed and established. Then why was Narendra Modi invited as a chief guest?" Hearing the words of that gentleman the Principal with his discreet smile said, "You have asked a very good question. Now you must hear the reply. It is not that I had not invited the big guns and prominent leaders for this important function. I wrote letters to all the great personalities of the country; they were phoned also. Some of them replied and some others neither sent a reply nor a word on phone till this day." That gentlemen listened to the words of the Principal with surprise. Then suddenly the Principal resumed with a smile, "I am still awaiting reply from a few others, now that our programme is coming to a close." At this that gentleman also smiled. Again the Principal spoke seriously, "Having written letters to those personalities I was waiting for their reply. Of them all I got the first reply from the office of Narendra Modi.

And see, I got the reply from him within fifteen minutes of my writing the invitation to him. Just think, Modiji's promptness to work and his capacity for quick decision. He is unparalleled in this respect. Within 15 minutes my staff contacted Narendra Modi and informed me. Narendra Modi's simplicity and happily accepting my invitation without any dallying appealed to our hearts so deeply. Today our country needs leaders like him. If there is anybody who can take our country to progress in every field, that man is Modiji and none else."

Principal's view about Modiji touched the man's heart very deeply. He also replied, "You are absolutely right and you will see one day Modiji will turn it into reality."

The words of the Principal along with that gentleman's proved true. Today Modiji with his policies and working skill is earning a great name for the country.

❑

Development Schemes of Gujarat

"Children, yesterday I told you that I would ask you about the development in Gujarat. Have you came prepared for it?" Ravi Madan said.

"Yes madam, we are fully prepared ", said Hetal.

"Bravo! Well Hetal, I begin with you. You tell me what are the important schemes of Gujarat?"

"Madam, the development schemes in Gurarat are Panchamrit Scheme, Sujlam Suflam, Krishi Mahotsava, Chiranjivi Scheme, Matri Vandana, Beti Bhachao, Jyoti Gram Scheme, Karmayogi Abhiyan, Kanya Kala Vani Sheme and Bal Bhog Scheme."

"Shabash, Hetal! You have named all the schemes." Thereafter, she told the class," Now I will ask each student to stand up and ask him/her to describe one of these schemes in one line each. The child who describes it correctly will be rewarded."

First of all she asked Ullas to stand up and asked, "Beta, what is Panchamrit Scheme?"

Ullas thought for a while and then said, "Madam, under this scheme there is the integrated five pronged development scheme so that the state may move forward towards development."

"Wah, a very good answer! Take your seat. Those who give correct answers will be rewarded in the end."

Now there was a competition among students to give the reply by raising their hands. Ravi said, "Now who will speak about Sujlam Suflam Scheme?" To speak about it, 20 hands of the children went up. She asked Simram sitting in the last row to stand up and speak. Thinking a bit Simram said, " Madam, under this scheme the water resources available in the state have been identified for their proper utilization so that wastage of water may be curbed and valuable water may be saved."

"Absolutely correct."

Gaurav put up his hand to speak about the next scheme, "Krishi Mahotsava". His father was a farmer, so he was supposed to have knowledge of agriculture. Ravi asked him to stand up and say about it. Gaurav said, "This scheme is designed to make agriculture improved and fertile."

"This, too, is correct. Now speak about Jyoti Gram Scheme."

This time Keshav spoke, "Madam, the aim of Jyoti Gram Scheme is to provide electricity to every home."

Mausam spoke about Beti Bachao, "The aim of this scheme is to prevent female foeticide to save the gird child."

"Perfectly true." Ravi said, "Now Amit will say about Matri Vandana."

Amit said, "The aim of this scheme is to safeguard the health of mother and child."

Ravi said, "All you children are very intelligent. I tell you about Kanya Kala Vani Scheme. The aim of this scheme is to promote female literacy and enlighten people about education in the state so that nobody is illiterate in the county."

Just then Ujjawala said, "Madam, you did not ask about Bal Bhog Scheme. Shall I speak about it?"

"Yes, yes, why not" !said Ravi

"Under Bal Bhog scheme the poor students are to be provided with food in schools so that their education is not hampered in the absence of food."

"Madam, I will speak about Karmayogi Abhiyan", said Anjana.

"Anjana's father was a government staff. She said, "This scheme has been designed to arouse sense of duty in government staff towards their work."

"Arre wah, class X is very intelligent. If all of you of this class go on pursuing your studies, then surely our state of Gujarat will write the new story of development in India," Ravi Madam said.

Just then the bell rang and giving best wishes to children Ravi Madam moved towards next class.

❑

Affection for Laxman

In Delhi there was a man to help Narendra Modi. His name was Laxman. Because of living with Narendra Modi for a long time he had deep affection for him. He was thoroughly impressed by Narendra Modi's ability and efficiency. One day Laxman was talking about Modiji with his colleague. Laxman said to his colleague, "Modiji is a man of immense ability and skill. Very soon he will reach a very high position with his labour. I have seen that while working he is fully absorbed in work, forgets everything else and minds only his work on hand.

The colleague said, "Yes, everybody has the same opinion about him. Only a man of passion reaches the highest position. But after reaching the top most position he will hardly remember small people like us."

"No, I don't think so. Modiji is simple hearted. He never forgets anybody, especially those with whom he meets and has daily intercourse with."

"Laxman, don't feel too happy. Your meeting with him is limited till he is here. After he goes away, he will forget you and get absorbed in new works."

"No, I don't agree to this also."

"You may not agree, later on you are sure to agree."

Days passed. At last the day came when it was decided to make Modiji Chief Minister of Gujarat. When Laxman got this news he could not contain his emotion and set out to see Modiji. There was a mammoth gathering at the swearing in ceremony. Laxman also reached the venue to extend his greetings to Modiji. He wrote a slip and somehow made it reach Modiji. Big VIPs were in the queue to see him. Laxman was at the farthest end of the line. Today he came to realise the truth of his friend's words. With sadness in his heart as he was to turn back from the line he heard his name called from the dais. Laxman was astonished to hear his name. On the dais it was announced, "Wherever Laxman is, he is wanted here, Narendra Modi wants to see him."

Hearing it Laxman was beside himself with joy. Tears welled up in his eyes. Going forward with folded hands before Narendra Modiji he said, "Saheb today is the most beautiful day of my life. I will not forget this moment till my death. Today I have got the wealth of a lifetime."

Narendra Modiji embraced Laxman. The big crowd was astonished to see Narendra Modi embracing Laxman. After that Narendra told Laxman, "I have received untold affection and intimacy from you. How can I forget you?"

Hearing it Laxman was beside himself with joy.

❑

Temple of Democracy

In 2014 Narendra Modi became Prime Minister of the country with absolute majority. The whole country along with reputed leaders were impatiently waiting for the new Prime Minister's arrival. At last the wait ended and Prime Minister Narendra Modi reached Parliament House for the first time. Parliament House was also waiting for him earnestly. As Narendra Modi reached the first step before entering Parliament House, he stopped. Others also stopped with him. Prime Minister Narendra Modi bent low and placing his head on the stair of Parliament House offered his salutation. While saluting the stairs his face showed peace and prayer.

Seeing the gesture, all leaders present were spell bound. Having saluted the stairs of Parliament House Narendra Modi accepted the greetings of all leaders. After that he touched the entrance gate with folded hands. He said, "I entered the chamber of Chief Minister of Gujarat for the first time when I was appointed Chief Minister of Gujarat. I also entered the assembly for the first time when I became Chief Minister of Gujarat. The parliament of our country is the 'temple of democracy'. As people wish fulfilment of their wishes and dreams in a temple, in the same way through the medium of the parliament it is our duty and responsibility to try to fulfil the dreams and wishes of democracy. Every person while entering parliament should entertain within him not only pious thoughts and emotions, rather he should perform his duty with labour and heart and soul. All of us who enter parliament know it full well that we have been sent here by the people to fulfil a particular responsibility. Along with security of the country our first duty should be to satisfy the democracy as a whole."

All leaders present there agreed with the words of Shri Narendra Modi. They said, "All of us sitting in the temple of democracy will ensure the security of the country and solve the problem of our countrymen."

Feeling satisfied with their resolve Shri Narendra Modi took up the charge of the country.

❑

Foreign Policy

Narendra Modi was victorious with a massive majority. He was to take oath as the Prime Minister. He had decided in his mind that he would give a new dimension to foreign policy. To take the country on to the path of progress it is necessary to forge amicable relations with neighbouring countries along with great powers. Thinking of such far reaching effects in his swearing-in-ceremony in 2014 as Prime Minister he invited the Heads of the States from South Asian countries. After swearing in he began his foreign tours with Bhutan. This initiative of Modiji had a positive effect and remarkable improvements were visible in India's relations with Asian countries. To promote the interests of India Modiji forged a strategy of foreign tours. Each foreign tour was opening up a new path of developing India's interests. Noticing it he said, "We have rule of law in India. The investor's money will not be allowed to sink. Therefore, investors should freely invest in India."

When he went on tour to Japan he told the citizens there, "In our country there is no 'red tape' rather there is a 'red carpet' spread for investors. Campaigns like Make in India and Digital India have established India as a brand. Naturally there is a day by day increase in foreign investment.

Not only this, India in 2015 has become the greatest country in the world to receive direct foreign investment."

One day a discussion was going on among learned people in the context of foreign policy. Placing his views Modiji said, "For the defense of the country the jawans of the Army are as much integral as is important the leadership of the country. India is not in favour of terrorizing any country nor is ready to take things lying down." Howsoever powerful a country, India is ready to go forward eye to eye and does not harbour any ambition to browbeat the other. We are not prepared to bow down. But India has the capacity to talk with the world eye to eye.

At these words of Modiji the people present there showed their agreement by clapping. A learned man said, "By improving relations with South East and Eastern Asian countries India is figuring as a great power. As such, each young person and people in general will have to tie up with the wave of development. When each young person will float in the wave of development, it will make India a super power and the country will be able to turn itself into heaven with its power and capability.

❑

Clean India Mission

"Mummy, mummy, today please celebrate my birth day at India Gate. I have asked all my friends to be present there. Cutting cake in the India Gate Park we will enjoy ourselves", Thirteen year old Pulkit said.

At 5 p.m. all assembled there. Pulkit was wearing very nice clothes. His friends were also in their best clothes. As a big cake was placed there, all friends there were elated. After cutting the cake Pulkit's parents gave pieces of cake to everybody. Thereafter, they were to take them to a good restaurant. Eating the cake hurriedly the friends threw away the plates hither and thither and got interested in playing. At a small distance from there a 14 year old boy Bhola was selling balloons. Bhola had just one leg. Perhaps he had lost another leg in some accident. When he saw that empty plates were lying about the place, he put his balloons on one side. He started collecting the plates by crawling around.

Pulkit saw him doing it. Pulkit thought that perhaps he was picking up the plates just to get some crumbs of the cake. He went to him and asked, "Will you have a cake?"

Bhola said smilingly, "No, Chhote Saheb, I don't want cake. These empty plates are sullying the beauty of the park as well as India Gate. So picking them up I am depositing them in the dustbin so that cleanliness of my country is maintained."

Pulkit was very much impressed to hear it. He felt very much ashamed of his action. He also started picking up the plates and dumping them into the dustbin. Now even the friends of Pulkit came up. Seeing the friends of Pulkit Bhola said, "It's good, you people realized your responsibility that we have to keep our country clean. We all know this thing that for the purpose of making India clean Prime Minister Modiji himself on 2 October, 2014 at Rajghat in Delhi had cleaned the street. The target of this mission is to reach cleanliness including toilet in every family by 2 October, 2019. If our country is clean the people living in villages and towns will be healthy and everybody will get clean eatables in sufficient quantity. To make this mission popular at global level by rousing the consciousness of general public the government had inspired the staff and officers of all government institutes on 2 October, 2014. Not only this, in order to take part in this mission several personalities related to the film industry came forward and became part of this programme. The objective of this mission is that the system of defecating in the open in the country should be rooted out because it creates nuisance and people fall sick more often. This scheme has joined all children like us with community health and cleanliness. If we dirty the public places, it means that we don't love our country."

Seeing Bhola speak continuously on Clean India Mission, Pulkit along with his father Rohan and mother Roma and friends were astonished. Pulkit asked sheepishly, "How do you have so much information?"

Bhola spoke with a smile, "Arre Bhai, I am also a student like you. I am also a school going boy. Now I am in class

VIII. I have only my sick mother at home. As such, I have to work to earn my livelihood. One day I lost my right leg in an accident. Do you know, I met with an accident because somebody had thrown a banana peel on the road? I did not see it, so I stepped on that peel, I slipped and fell and a car ran over me."

Hearing it all children's eyes including those of Pulkit became moist. Pulkit asked, "Will you be my friend?"

Bhola spoke smilingly, "Friend already, don't you see I have been picking up empty plates thrown by you just to clean the place."

Hearing it a smile ran over Pulkit's face and he held Bhola a piece of cake to this mouth. Thereafter they all promised Bhola that they would become part of Clean India Mission and would contribute their utmost to keep the country clean.

❑

Postage Stamp on Modi

It was Navya's sixteenth birth day. She was very happy. She had invited all friends of her class. After cutting the cake congratulations along with gifts began to pour in. Accepting everyone's greetings Navya would keep the gifts on one side. Then came her favourite friend Bhavya. Bhavya also had a gift in her hand, Navya knew that Bhavya always gave her some special gift, so she wanted to see her gift first. This time when Bhavya gave her gift she did not forget to add, "Navya, you must open it only after eating your dinner. Otherwise if you open it just now, you will not feel interested in the party."

Hearing the words of Bhavya, Navya began to wait restlessly to open that gift. All friends had their dinner and began to take leave of her. She told Bhavya, "You please wait. Your flat is adjacent to mine. Papa will escort you home. Also tomorrow is Sunday. You will not be in a hurry to go to school." It was about 10 o'clock. Seeing Navya restlessness Bhavya phoned her mummy that she would be home by eleven o' clock.

After that Navya and Bhavya started picking up the gifts and keeping them in Navya's room. When all gifts were arranged she first of all opened Bhavya's gift and she jumped out of joy as she opened it. Bhavya had given Navya a postage stamp issued on Narendra Modi in Turkey. Seeing such a valuable gift Navya embraced Bhavya. She said, "Tell me, how could you perform such a difficult task? I had different postage stamps, but in fact, I had a desire to include this stamp in my collection. You have fulfilled my desire."

Bhavya said with a smile, "I am your bosom friend. I know every little thing about you. When Modiji had arrived in Turkey in 2015 to take part in leaders' G-20 Summit and the President of Turkey Resep Tayeep had presented different postage stamps of the leaders present there, since then I had the desire to procure the postage stamp anyhow for you. My brother Sahil had gone to Turkey in connection with his business. I had asked him to bring the postage stamp at any cost. Now how could my brother disappoint me?"

"Wah Bhavya, this gift of yours hasstupefied me. I know in the G-20 Summit conference it was for the first time that 33 postage stamps were issued of which 19 postage stamps were of big and powerful leaders of the world."

"Yes, Navya! We consider issuing postage stamp on Prime Minister Modiji is a matter of pride for us Indians." Navya's eyes were still locating the fineness of the postage stamp.

Bhavya said, "Where are you? Is madam feeling sleepy?"

"Arre no, I'm not sleepy. I have noticed that this stamp also has our national flag. Just see-" Navya said showing the stamp to Bhavya.

Bhavya saw that the stamp had the picture of Narendra Modi and India's national flag printed on the stamp. Seeing it Bhavya said, "This stamp has been issued in the currency of Turkey."

"Yes Bhavya ! I will store this postage stamp in my collection of postage stamps."

Just then the clock struck eleven. Bhavya said, "Arre, both of us were absorbed in the postage stamp, we did not open other gifts to see them."

Navya said, "Tomorrow is Sunday. Come early morning and have your breakfast here. After that, we will see the other gifts."

"All right."

Bhavya thenwent her home and Navya got up to store the stamp on Modi in her collection of postage stamps.

❑

Digital India

"Rinku I had to go to pay the mobile bill, but I could not do so until now. Today you will go to the mobile centre and pay my bill."

"Uncle, how much is your bill?"

"It is eight hundred fifty rupees."

"Okay."

Thereafter Rinku opened his mobile and switched on its data. He took some time and then said, "Uncle, your bill has been paid. Now do your work peacefully."

Seeing it Ajay uncle looked at Rinku with surprise and said, "Arre, sitting at home how was the bill paid? When I go to the centre to pay the bill, it takes half an hour to one hour."

"Yes, uncle, now you will utilize your time in increasing the agricultural produce. Perhaps you are not aware of Prime Minister Narendra Modi's Digital India Mission."

"Yes my son, tell me about it."

"Uncle, this mission was started by Prime Minister Modiji on 1 July 2015. The aim of this scheme is to develop the people of the country more. From this scheme the people of the country will have untold advantages. For example, even in the villages the digital facility has been started. Just because of that the bill was paid. Otherwise one had to go to the centre to pay the bill. Uncle, from digital operation there will be less paper work and all works will be done through electronic gadgets. It will minimize consumption of paper and will curb pollution. At the same time in order to save your time you can take advantage of e- hospital, e-banking etc. in a short time. Digital India is such a programme under which the target is to connect with broad band about 2.5 lakh Panchayats along with six lakh villages. By now several thousand panchayats have been connected with this scheme. Not only this, uncle, Prime Minister Narendra Modi has a dream that Indian farmers should get the benefit of I.T. Sectors. For this action is being taken to connect agricultural produce, details regarding transaction and the details of selling price etc. Under this programme the government wants to establish digital service in each village so that all people may be provided with government services and maximum people may take advantage of it."

"Beta, but those who are not much educated, how will they take advantage of it?"

"Arre uncle, it is not a difficult task. A little practice does the thing. Under this scheme online approach will be made to information and documents. From it, people will easily receive information and in a way there will be a two way communication between the government and the people which will restrain corruption, too."

"Beta, at present I am not able to fully understand your words."

"Doesn't matter uncle, so long as I am here with you, I will be giving you information every day. From it you will clearly have knowledge of these things and then you will yourself be an expert in handling digital transactions."

"Okay, Beta. I will try to learn it whole heartedly."

After that Ajay went away to work in his field and Rinku started writing notes for Ajay uncle in simple language to give him information regarding Digital India.

❑

A Gift of Books

Once Narendra Modi came in a programme wherepeople gave him gifts of several bouquets of flowers. Some bouquets were very costly. They had costly flowers woven into them. The flowers were spreading their fragrance all around. Seeing bouquet all around several guests talked among them, "The gift of bouquet is such as it is spreading its fragrance all around. It refreshes the man who presents as well as others present around. The fragrance and colour of fresh flowers cast a magic like spell and play an important role in dispelling one's pain and suffering."

A woman standing there said, "Of course! That's why in our culture it is meet to present a bouquet to a sick person so that the sick person may get up from the bed fresh as a flower and it may bring smile on the face of the people around him."

Hearing such words a man who had deep knowledge of the variety of flowers began to express his views. He said, "Absolutely correct. I totally agree with you people. The bright colour of bougainvillea, the rainbow colour of chrysanthemum, lotus and dahlia flowers is a thing exceptional. A mere look at them gives coolness to the eyes. "Now there ensued a discussion on the bouquet of flowers in the programme. But none of the people present there said that there could be a better gift than a bouquet of flowers. Narendra Modi heard all people's views. He said," All of you people have good knowledge of flowers. It is a good thing. True, a bouquet of flowers is a very good gift. But there is a gift even more precious which I hesitate to offer. I will rather say that the bouquet of flowers later and that gift should be given first."

Hearing it a man told Modiji, "Sir, which gift?"

Modiji replied smilingly, "Arre, none other than books. I am talking about books. Many poets and writers hold that books talk to them, they lead the way to life and protect them against all odds. As such what other gifts can be better than that which lives with us like a friend throughout our life, shows a new path and takes our life to new heights." Hearing Modiji all people present there were astonished. Really what Modiji had said was true. Books are not only one's true friend but also one's guide. All people present there endorsed the view of Modiji. Some people even took a pledge that wherever they go with a gift they will present only the most valuable gift of books so that the country may go forward on the path of progress.

❑

Yogah Karmsu Kaushalam

One day Narendra Modi was talking sitting with some senior people in a meeting. The talk was about people's self-respect and job. An old man said, "Beta, there are many things of my generation which when I tell my grandchildren today, my heart is filled with pride. In my age people were true to their word, deed and faith. They honoured their commitment even at the cost of their life."

Several other people narrated their similar experiences. A woman told Modiji, "Saheb, has anything happened in your life which you have not forgotten as yet and feel proud to narrate it?"

Hearing the words of the woman Modiji was lost in past memories. After thinking for a moment he said, " My sister, though there are several memories which I can never forget in my life."

Hearing it all people said in one voice, "Please tell us about that incident. We all want to hear it."

Modiji said, "Once I was travelling by train from Vadnagar. Suddenly a few minutes later a young boy entered my compartment. He was polio-affected. He struggled and somehow entered the compartment. All eyes turnedto him. Passengers thought that he would go to them to beg for alms. As soon as he approached a person, he started looking towards his shoes. All people thought that perhaps he wanted a pair of shoes to put on. The man wearing shoes began to look at the young man with surprise. From his dirty and tattered clothes he took out a small box of polish and a brush and looking towards the gentleman said, "Sa'b boot polish, I will polish your shoes for fifteen rupees." The gentleman agreed. Hearing it the young man was filled with zeal and self-confidence. He took out a newspaper from his bag and held it to that gentleman. The gentleman took the newspaper with surprise. On it in very fine hand words were written, "Wish you a happy journey. May your journey be auspicious and your mission be fulfilled." Reading it the customer became very pleased. He started turning over the pages of the newspaper. The gentleman told other people, "Wah, it is a very good thing. With best polish for fifteen rupees I am getting worth one rupee newspaper free." Now, others also started asking him to polish their shoes. I was watching all this. Then that young man said, "I am from Karnataka. I have none in my family. Being invalid physically I am unable to do any job but I don't want to live on other's charity by begging. I want to work for the people, for the county. Therefore every morning before I go out I buy a newspaper for a rupee and on that paper I write with my pen good wishes for the travellers. This way for twenty to thirty people I give them the newspaper to read while I polish their shoes. Thus I live a respectful life."

After narrating it Modiji told the people in the meeting, "That day I came to realize that the words written in the "Geeta" mean what that boy was demonstrating with his word and deed. Yogah Karmsu Kaushalam is that very thing which that young man was practising every day. Alas! Every

Indian could imbibe in him thespirit of " Yougah Karmsu Kausalam" to make the county go forward on the path of success faster and faster."

Hearing the words of Modiji all people who were present there had their eyes moist. They said, "All of us will try to live with dignity as long as we live."

Modiji smiled to hear them.

❑

A Nice Journey by Metro

One day Narendra Modi was talking with his select persons about the traffic in Delhi. Everybody was narrating his own experience with traffic in Delhi. A man said, "Sir, the roads of Delhi look less wide and more congested today. Previously the traffic during noon time was less but today anytime there is a jam and overcrowding due to which one has to face a lot of inconvenience."

Another man said, "I also agree with you. Seeing the crowd of vehicles on the roads of Delhi it seems that if people had their say, they would jam the roads even in the night."

A third man said, "Yes, all this is true. Now at the call of the time people have become too busy. The work style has also been changing day to day. The standard of people is rising. Previously having a car in a family was a big thing now in many houses each member has his own car. They go out on road in their own car at their own time. So, the roads are every time crowded. It increases pollution and pollutes the air as well as sound".

Modiji listened to everybody. Then he said, "All of you are right. But there is no problem in the world of which no solution can be found. As a problem arises from somewhere, similarly the same problem comes to an end somewhere.

In our country in several states the metro rail has provided easy travel and created a good name for itself. Travelling by metro has many advantages. Protecting yourself against sun, shower and cold you can enjoy the travelling by metro. It saves time. There is no inconvenience of road jam there. The metro train comes every minute so that the traveller reaches his destination within the stipulated time. I myself find metro travel very pleasant. So from time to time I enjoy metro travel with common people. Not only this, when I get an opportunity. I also inspire my foreign guest to enjoy the metro in our country. It strengths our social and economic condition. If people make more use of the public transport in place of their own vehicle, it will make Delhi not only clean and beautiful, but it will also reduce consumption of petroleum products. It will also save natural resources in our country for the coming generation. That's why all people should understand these things and travel by public transport and also take care of them".

Hearing his words the people present there said, " Sir, we will also use metro from time to time and make our Delhi and India clean and pollution free by contributing our best."

Hearing these words the usual smile returned over the face of Modiji and he said, "This is also our motto- with all, for all."

❑

Pranks during Marriages

On Teacher's Day Narendra Modi was talking to children. Seeing children even elderly people start visualising their childhood. Modiji was talking to children in their own tone. Children were asking him child-like questions to which he was giving the answer with a smile. A child said, "Sir, in childhood children indulge in naughty acts and at several acts they are rebuked by their parents. Did you not commit any such mischief for which you were scolded?"

Hearing such a question of that child Narendra Modi had a smile on his lips. He said, "Childhood is meant for mischief. What childhood is that in which a child does no mischief"?

At this another child said, "Sir, you also tell us some incident for which you were rebuked by elders."

At this all children cried in one voice, "Yes, yes Sir, please tell us, please. We want to hear about your childhood pranks."

Hearing the words of children Modiji began to think and recall incidents of his childhood. Suddenly he remembered an incident and a smile spread over his lips. He said, "I have also committed several pranks. But when grown up it comes to mind that had I not committed some of those pranks, it would have been better. I will tell you about one such incident of my life, but first you will have to promise me that you will not commit that mischief which I had done in my childhood."

All children promised not to do any mischief which might cause damage or suffering to people. Modiji said, "My friend circle had many friends. When our friend circle went to any marriage or barat party, we never refrained from doing mischief there. During marriage when the moment of garland exchange would come, all people would see that programme sitting. Then my friends and I would become active and alert to execute our plan. We could sit with a safety pin with us and would attach it to the clothes of others. The garland exchange and tilak programmes took a long time, so for long they did not know that their clothes had been linked with others' clothes. After linking their clothes we would stealthily slip away from there and would see the fun from a distance. After the programme when those people would try to get up their clothes would be linked with other's. In such a situation one would move left and the other right. And we would laugh to see their embarrassment."

Hearing it all children started laughing boisterously.

Modiji said, "Children, now you may laugh to hear it, but you will not at all practise it, because now I realize that by chance it may prick the person or other person so linked may dash against something causing him damage or hurt."

All children said, "Sir, we will never practise a mischief and while doing any mischief we will make sure that it does not cause any damage or hurt anybody."

Modiji became very pleased to hear the words of children. He said, "Bravo my children! You are very wise. Study carefully and go ahead. You have my blessings." ❑

A Scheme to Develop Villages

One day a discussion was on in a meeting of leaders. Prime Minister Narendra Modi was drawing a blue print for the development of the whole country. There it was noticed that even the basic facilities like electricity, water and toilet are not available in many villages today. The development of villages is a distant proposition, the greater part of the villagers' time is spent in solving the problem of electricity and water. In this context a study of villagers was made and it was found that several villagers did not have the facility of day to day requirements. Having come to know this Narendra Modi said, "Several years have passed since independence, but the dreams of Mahatma Gandhi could not be fulfilled. The soul of India lives in villages. Therefore it was Gandhiji's main aim to develop the villages. Now on the analogy of 'Smart City' the decision will be taken to develop a "Smart Village". Only then we can do justice with the dream of Gandhiji. Under 'M.P.'s model village scheme' full attention will be paid to the development of villages. The objective of this scheme is to establish those values in villages and their people so that they can be model villages for others. A model village means such a village which along with basic facilitiesmay be in the forefront of education, health and employment. This scheme is public oriented and it will be achieved through the guidance of M.P.'s and public co-operation. For this many M.Ps will have to adopt such villages where improvement is badly needed." Saying this Narendra Modi stopped for a minute. Thinking something he decided to adopt himself a village called Jayapur 25 km away from Banaras. At the same time he told his MPs not to adopt those villages inhabited by their relatives. That village will be adopted which is not even distantly related to any MP. With their insight and labour they will make that village "Smart Village" and will bring in other villages of the country on the path of progress. Only then the soul of India will be alive."

After that work in full swing started on this scheme. Journalist Lokendra Singh says that his maternal grand-mother's house Piprauna is situated at a distance of 25 km from Gwalior in Madhya Pradesh. Only three to four years ago it was difficult to reach there during rains. Now go to the village anytime, there is a no problem. From city to village there is good road link. There is also facility of water. There is a toilet in every house. Electricity supply is also there." In this way even villages are moving on the path of development and the whole country woven in a single string is on towards development.

❑

Modi, the Technoleader

One day while connecting the development of the country with technology Modi said, "Today technology has far advanced, WhatsApp, Twitter, Facebook and Instagram messages can be communicated with foreign countries within seconds. We will have to make this technology our weapon. I had understood that the future would belong totechnology, so I started learning and using this technology with gusto. You must have seen that in August 2012 through Google Hangout, I had a talk with the youth and all others in this connection. The people present there said, "Sir, you have said it perfectly! Now a days by 6 o'clock in the morning the newspaper becomes stale."

At this Modi said smilingly, "Absolutely! You know that for a long time I have been reading the news at 4 a.m on computer while taking tea. In this way before I start my work for the day I have knowledge of the world."

Seeing the discussion on technology going on another person said, "You have been interacting with the public through 'Swagat online' programme since 2004. Swagat i.e. state wide attention on grievances by application of technology that is, through technology the programme of grievances application. Through video conference you can speak to them right from your office with the people at village, sub division and district level, hear their grievances and also solve them."

Modiji said, "65% population of our country is youth. Today youth are connected with social media. Through social media one's say, complaint or problem can be communicated very easily. Therefore I have my website www.narendramodi.in in order to make a wide outreach. Making time out of my busy schedule, I must write. This website is available in all languages of the country, to the extent that it is available in Sanskrit, our most ancient language. Now new techniques are pouring in day by day and replacing the old techniques. You might have heard of the 3Dtechnology. Through this one can address people at different locations and at the same time one's speech can be communicated to far off places. Now even the 3D holographic projection technique is gaining momentum." Noticing Modiji's deep knowledge of technology a gentleman said, "Sir, your talent is unparalleled. It is the wonder of your skill and wisdom that the country is marching ahead with technology on the path of progress. That's why Mark Zuckerberg, the father of Facebook is seen making the remark, "If somebody has to learn how to perform something with the help of technology, he should look at the Prime Minister Narendra Modi of India and learn from him." What can be a better compliment than this for our country!' Modiji said smilingly, "It can be when our country stands among the super powers as their head and each country salutes her, then it will be a great thing for all of us."

All learned people present there agreed with Modiji and turned to their respective work.

❑

Blood Donation

One day Prime Minister Narendra Modi visited a Blood Donation Camp. There many people were donating their blood out of their own will. Seeing it Narendra Modi was greatly pleased. He called the blood donor. A blood donor said, "I certainly donate blood every six months or once a year. I know it well that blood donation does not cause weakness. So all of us healthy people should make it a routine to donate blood. As going on a tour regularly, exercising and eating food with all nutritious ingredients our body keeps healthy, in the same way by donating blood a man keeps healthy physically and mentally.

Modi felt very pleased to hear the words of the young man and said, "The country needs young men like you. The country has high hopes from young men filled with new thought and new energy."

Just then a young girl who had just donated blood said, "Sir, I also tell my friends at the college that young people above the age of eighteen must donate blood regularly. A few of my friends say that donating blood causes weakness. I tell them it is just a myth. It is not a fact."

Hearing the words of the young girl Narendra Modi said, "You are right. That's why I say that every person should be educated and have a clear mind. It is said that charity must be secret. Very often people donate so that their name should be written on the name-board but real donation is one that is made in a secret way and nobody has a scent of it. From this point of view blood donation is the great donation and also secret. From this donation one cannot know the religion, gender and caste of the donor. Thus, blood donation strengthens the foundation of unity and love and promotes brotherhood. Today I am very happy to see the outlook of young men in such a big number and I hope and believe that the future of India in the safe hands.

At this word of Modiji all young people said with a smile, "Sir, we are ever ready to sacrifice all for the country."

❑

Digital Payment as Mass Movement

One day Narendra Modi was making new plans for the development of the country. A learned man told Modiji, "Sir, now digital payment has caught up with the people in India. Yesterday I went to market just to have a taste of it. I noticed that many fruit and vegetable sellers had with them the facility of card and Paytm. Not only this, I also noticed that the young people right from the age of 18 to 78 have become part of digital payment."

Another leader was sitting there. He said, "Perfectly true. I have also marked more or less the same thing. There is a gentleman in my neighborhood named Ramlubhaya. Though he was an Accounts Officer in a government office but he had no knowledge of digital payment. His children are posted abroad. Now he had some problems at certain places. In the situation an N.C.C. cadet taught him how to make payment through the digital system. Now he comfortably works through card and Paytm and says really digital India is developed India." Hearing his words Modiji was smiling. He said, "Digital payment will have to be made mass movement. From now, young men of 15 to old men of 70 are making digital payments. It is a very encouraging thing. I have also announced several rewarding plans connected with the digital plan. On completion of those plans when people will be getting prizes, it will become more encouraging.

If a prize is added to a work, it becomes somewhat like bonus with remuneration and inspires people to work with more energy and freshness. I want that 1.25 crore Indians should be connected with Bhim App and go ahead with digital currency. It will develop our country both in technology and industry very fast. Behind making digital payment a mass movement my aim is to educate each and every Indian."

Hearing the words of Modiji all people bowed their heads in reverence and said, "Sir, through digital payment everyone will become educated and the lamp of education will light each home."

❑

Earthen Lamp

Once Pawan Acharya of Albert sent a message to Prime Minister Narendra Modi. He wrote "My name is Pawan Acharya and I am from Alwar in Rajasthan. I want to request Prime Minister Narendra Modiji that this time in your 'Man Ki Baat' please call upon the public of India to use earthen lamps on Deepawali as much as possible. It will benefit environment as well as the potter brothers will get a job."

Modi took this message seriously. He liked the suggestion of Pawan very much. Making an appeal to the public he said, "I believe that with the speed of wind this feeling will surely reach every corner of India. Pawan has given a good suggestion. Earth is invaluable, it is most valuable. Therefore the earthen lamps are also invaluable. Even today in the twenty-first century bulb & tube light cannot compete with the eastern lamp because even today man cannot light from one tube light to another tube light, whereas from one earthen lamp numerous lamps can be lighted and spread light all around. Earthen lamp is a symbol of light, riches and love. Light has been regarded as the symbol of soul, brahma and knowledge. It is also a symbol of spiritual and physical joy and progress. So you must include an earthen lamp in life apart from Deepawali. When we look at the light of an earthen lamp in peace, we find a lot to learn. It removes the darkness of our mind and lightens the inner spark. Earthen lamp is an ideal of our light, it is the condition of life, the lesson of refinement and inspiration for resolve. Try to pass on this lesson and inspiration to children. By doing this the light of numerous lamps will spread and then our country will develop by lea and bounds and this light will suggest everyone that the civilization and culture of India is comparable to none." Hearing these words of Prime Minister Narendra Modi many people have started lighting earthen lamps every night. Some people place the earthen lamp at dark places so that it may light the paths to the traveller and spread light in his innermost chamber.

□

Respect the Army

Narendra Modi had gone to see the army on the border where he saw the bravery and zeal of the army fighting on the border and saluted them. Once he visited such a camp where new recruits were being given training. Seeing the hard training Modiji said, "The army is given inordinately hard training. That's why some people are afraid of it."

The officers said, "Sir, in military such training is a must. This training is called "Boot Camp". Under this "Boot Camp" people are trained in discipline and practice; this training is very tough, so sometimes the weak ones leave it mid-way and accept their defeat, but the strong minded ones easily overcome the Boot Camp and sacrifice their all for the country." Modiji was watching the training and practice very closely. When he returned from there the fact was hovering in his mind how the army living in camps away from their family without caring about their life undergo such training. Once he went to address a rally. There a large crowd was very eager to listen to him. He welcomed the crowd with a smile. He said, "All of you see how our army men careless of sun, cold and snow are true to the their duty. Our soldiers are not afraid of death. Because of the army standing on the borders we live comfortably in our homes. Today I want that all of you should take a resolve in your heart that whenever you see an army man, you will stand up in respect and welcome him by clapping. By doing this our army brothers will feel encouraged; they will feel good that every Indian respects their work, appreciates it, won't you do it?"

Hearing these words of Modiji all hands in the crowd went up and with clapping came the words. "We will surely respect our army brothers. Not only this, in the absence of our unknown brothers we will care for their family."

Hearing the public Modiji said, "When people have an attitude like this, rest assured our India will step further and march towards becoming a super power.

❑

Surgical Strike

A 70 year old Sardar Singh watching TV said, "O God! How long will these terrorist attacks go on killing our soldiers?" Sardar Singh himself had been a soldier. Seeing his patriotic zeal and passion even today people could not help admiring him and calling him 'jawan'.

On TV the news was going on. The news reader was announcing that in Uri sector of Jammu and Kashmir in a suicidal terrorist attack on the 12 base 17 jawans were killed. The army has killed all the four terrorists. This sinister attack was made at 5.15 in Uri of Baramulla when all soldiers were sleeping in their tents. According to available sources, during the attack the jawans, of the Dogra regiment were sleeping in a tent which caught fire as a result of explosion. The fire spread to the adjacent barracks. It is believed that the terrorists infiltrated into the camp before making the attack."

Sardar Singh switched off the TV. It was the morning of 18thSeptember 2016.

Outside the neighbours too, were condemning the attack. In the evening while talking Mr Chopra said, "What would have been the condition of those houses of the attack victims. Tell me, do the terrorist have no feelings in their hearts. How could they have committed such a heinous act?

Sardar Singh said, "Hearing of such attacks of terrorists my blood boils. We must never forgive them. It is essential to give them hardest possible punishment. But I think now our Prime Minister will certainly take some very hard action. Let me see, what is the TV saying now?" After that Mr. Chopra also came in with Sardar Singh. On TV news channel the news reader was saying, "Along with Prime Minister Modi the whole world has vehemently condemned the attack." The Prime Minister has said that he assures the country that the culprits will not be spared.

After that not only Sardar Singh but the whole country was looking ferocious against the terrorists. Now in each Indian's heart the feeling of patriotism had came to the fore. Prime Minister Modi was also petrified from this incident. He asked the Indian army to give a befitting response to the terrorist attack.

On 29th September Sardar Singh was talking to his neighbour Mr Chopra when his daughter Rakhi turned the TV on. Suddenly watching the news on TV Sardar Singh and Mr Chopra along with the whole country could not help appreciating the step taken by Narendra Modi. By instigating surgical strike he had given a befitting reply to terrorists.

Watching it Mr. Chopra asked, "What's Surgical Strike?"

Sardar Singh explained, "Surgical Strike is such an attack in which only selected targets are destroyed. Under this attack besides the target the security of public is ensured so that innocent people are not harmed or inconvenienced."

"Arre, wah, really our Prime Minister is so wise. He respects every individual. That's why he went on a strategy to punish only the guilty. Otherwise our neighbour does not hesitate to harm the general public while executing their nefarious activities."

"Arre Choprajee, that's why Prime Minister Modiji has carved out an exclusive image for himself in the world." I feel that through Modiji our country is not only on the path of self defence but also eager to link the whole world to himself."

"What you have said is perfectly true."

"Just then Rakhi came up with tea and said, "Uncle please have tea and Pakodas on the success of the surgical strike."

Chopra and Sardar Singh started eating Pakodas along with tea and were engaged in discussion again.

❑

Silent Revolution

Through "Man ki Baat" Prime Minister Narendra Modi had linked the general public with himself. Till now a work or scheme reached the far off villages very late, but through radio "Man ki Baat" each citizen was connected with the Modi's mind. Modi started communicating his thoughts every month in "Man ki Baat" programme being broadcast on the radio. Through the medium of radio itself he appealed to the rich people in every home to take part in "Ujjwala Yojna". Now we are in a country where the food will be cooked not on earthen stove but on gas stove. That time saved should be applied not to cooking food but to making new schemes. There is poverty in villages even today because the development scheme reaches there too late. We have to strengthen the villages. Every village has to be connected with telephone, education, electricity and gas cylinder. In such a state the able and affluent people just by forgoing gas subsidy without doing any labour can become invisible part of social service. From the subsidy forgone by you it will become easy to provide the facilities to those poor people who don't have money to buy even two square meals. When he gets gas cylinder free of charge, it will become easy for him to cook food. In this way their time which was spent on procuring firewood will now be devoted to constructive works. At the same time women will be protected against several diseases. The smoke from earthen stove and chimney causes them cough and other diseases which makes them sick. In our country it is essential for everybody to be healthy. I want to see them healthy. Only healthy hands can contribute to the progress of the country. So, everybody has to be healthy not only for himself but also for others and do for them what he can easily do."

Countless people heard this appeal of Modiji and several people voluntarily gave up subsidy on gas cylinder. The subsidy forgoer includes not only the rich families, but also retired teachers, widows, army men and old ones, too. Noticing it Modiji thanking each such citizen said that in reality our country is transforming, going ahead. It is a silent revolution which is manifesting itself in development.

❑

The Fashion of Khadi

"Arre, Jigna, what's the matter? Today you have put on a beautiful Khadi kurta over your jeans. Wah, where did you buy, my friend?" Said Kaimreena.

"Today I had been to Delhi Haat. There I liked it and bought it. Anyway now I am thinking of buying some Khadi Kurta. Not only this, I want to buy Khadi bag and other Khadi items as well."

"Why so Jigma? This sudden Khadi love where from?" Vipul asked

Just recalling something Gautam said, "O, madam, now I have understood. Perhaps our Jigna madam has heard that appeal of our Prime Minister, in which he had advised all people to adopt Khadi. Wah yaar ! Really you're the winner, Jigna. I had also heard the words of Modiji he was saying that when our country was dependent, all Indians were earnestly trying to make use of Indian products. They were not afraid of boycotting costly foreign goods. Seeing the spirit and enthusiasm of Indians the Englishmen's morale went on declining. At last they had to leave India lock, stock and barrel. Then every Indian said to another Indian, 'Khadi for nation'. This Khadi for nation was the need of the time then, in the modern times I would like to ask the youth whether 'Khadi for nation' should not apply now?"

Seeing Gautam repeating the words of Modiji students looking at him with surprise said, "Yaar, we are afraid, you didn't prepare that appeal yourself? You are repeating word by word."

Sankalp said, "Arre Yaar, you all know that Gautam does not miss any speech or even the tiniest news about Modiji. After all, he is the President of the college."

Jigna said, 'True yaar, Modi's words are very inspiring. Modiji had also said that he does not say that we should wear all khadi clothes only. I only say that of your many cloth sets one set must be of khadi. When we 1.25 crore countrymen buy any khadi or handloom item of 5 to 10 rupees or 50 rupees, this money goes to a poor weaver. In the khadi business most of the weavers are poor. As such, when you buy one khadi set among many other sets, the poor man's bread is managed, their children have something to eat. If all Indians include some khadi clothes in their clothing, then it will not take long to dispel poverty from the country."

Now people started looking at Jigna with wonder. Sankalp said, "Jigna you also follow Modiji like Gautam."

"Arre, why shouldn't we follow, when Modiji feels so much concernfor young people. He says everything with an eye on the youth. Then it also becomes our duty to contribute all for the good of the country."

Hearing their words Kaimreena said, "Jigna yaar, I have been very much impressed by your and Gautam's words. You please advise me one or two dresses of fine khadi. After classes I will go with you.

Jigna said, "Of course." Thereafter she spoke with determination, "You should also follow me. You want to become a journalist. A journalist often wears khadi kurta. If you practise right now, it will be easier for you in the future."

At this all burst out laughing and the feeling of patriotism began rushing in their veins.

❑

Modi Wave

After inducting NDA's Chief Minister in Uttar Pradesh, Manipur and Goa. Modiji was being admired everywhere for his work. Ten to twelve intellectuals had to prepare a report on the progress of the country. It included Aman, Naman, Riya, Aisani, Vaishnavi, Illisha, Aayush, Aryan, Pankhuri and Saurya. Aisani said, "Let's have tea and while having tea we will analyze the progress made by the government."

Hearing the words of Aisani Vaishnavi and Saurya said cheerfully, " Wah, very nice! It's a very good idea."

Aman said," By doing so we can prepare a good development report of India."

They came to a café. There they ordered tea. Illisha said, "Let's have some snacks with tea."

Naman ordered tea and snacks. In a short while all friends began the discussion while sipping tea. Aayush said, "The Modi government with its work and decisions has shown how the country is led on to the path of development." Aryan said, "You are right. On 8 November 2016 when Modiji had decided on demonetization, since then it seemed that people would not like this decision of Modiji." At this Pankhuri said, "Yes, all of us had to stand in a queue before a bank."

Ilisha said, "Pankhuri, do you remember the struggle of

that period when in the ATM line by the time your number came, cash was exhausted."

Pankhuri added, "And madam, you tell us your story, every day you stood in line before a bank as if you were filling in form for the Miss India contest. You also used to set Vikas in the line since morning and yourself come prepared later. And the poor man became poorer standing in line." Seeing it Aishni said, "Well, here we have come to discuss progress of the country and not the progress of you two."

All laughed at it. Vaishnavi said, "Just see, all of us faced the trouble at that time, but not onlyus, even the poor to protest people liked this decision of the Prime Minister". Aishni said, "For full five months the whole country had to face problems, the economy had crashed but the Modi government very skillfully handled everything. Under Ujjwala Yojana by giving L.P.G. free of cost to the poor sections the country developed and countless women were freed from smoke."

Pankhuri said. "Yes, this is true. From chimney smoke women were victim to several diseases. Now many women cook food on gas stove very easily and save their time. Such women are running their business on gas stove and are adopting Modi's schemes like Start Up and Skill Development Scheme."

Aryan said, "At present no other leader is as dedicated, and laborious as Modiji can be seen anywhere. Aishni said, "I read newspaper and journals very closely. In the country's development there is unprecedented contribution of Modiji's super skill, marketing branding and dedication." Vaishnavi said "Aishni, what you say is perfectly correct. Our Prime Minister established contact with the public in a fine way." Alisa said, "In fact his contact with people is visible from his

Mann ki Baat in which many people share their thoughts with him and Modiji also carries his thoughts throughout the country through the radio show that every person may feel that he very close to Modiji."

Meanwhile the young brigades' tea had been over. Naman said, "Really along with the progress of the country I notice one thing clearly."

"What's that?" All asked seriously.

"Only that I and other boys are listening to the pleas of you girls and are silent ourselves. It also shows that Modiji has given a platform to women to place their views." Hearing it Aishni said with swagger, "O see, Modiji right from the beginning has been regarding women as superior to men. In fact, there are a few women who want to equal to men who do not know that women are far ahead of men."

Vaishnavi, Pankhuri, Alisha and Riya endorsed this view. Then all in one voice said, "The Modi wave is also visible on us since India has been taking firm decisions."

❑

Ujjwala Schemes

"Tai, when you cook food on stove, my eyes begin to water because of smoke and I feel restless. God knows how you continue with the habit of cooking food in smoke." - said Gaurav.

"Beta, I don't live in Delhi like you. Here all cook their food on stove. You already know that here are poor families like me. How can there be a gas stove to us. You have come here just for a few days. Have hot loaves from my earthen stove. You may not get such food in Delhi."

"Tai, in Delhi the finest food is available and you will be surprised to know that today I have come to liberate you from the earthen stove."

Ramawati Tai spoke with astonishment, "Arre beta, this earthen stove will leave me only after my death."

"Tai, today in the evening you will collect all women of the village. Today I will free them from earthen stoves who spend their whole life in smoke and fall a prey to serious diseases."

In the evening at the home meeting all women of the neighbourhoodgathered.

Gaurav spoke to them, "How many of you women cook food on earthen stove?"

Barring three to four women the rest raised their hands.

So many women are destroying their lives in smoke. Seeing it Gaurav heaved a deep sigh and said, "You must have known Modiji. Our Prime Minister is initiating new schemes. One of them is-Ujjwala Scheme. This scheme has been made for poor families of India. It was started by the government on 1stMay 2016. Under this scheme the Government of India has started to provide 5 crore L.P.G. connection free of cost to those families living below poverty line. It is an important scheme being run by the petroleum and natural gas Ministry of the Government of India. So, under this scheme to poor people like you L.P.G. will be made available free of cost."

Hearing the words of Gaurav a woman named Bhartari said, "It is a very good thing. But why is the government giving us gas connection free of charge? What is the government's design behind it?"

"You have asked a very good question"- said Gaurav and added, "The main purpose of this scheme is to promote L.P.G. in place of fossil fuel for cooking food in rural areas. At the same time there is another purpose to promote women's empowerment and ensure safety of health for persons like you. When you cook food from fossil fuel, many harmful gases enter your body which cause several diseases due to which many women die at a young age."

Hearing the words of Gaurav all women discussing among them said, "What Gaurav is saying is true. When I start cooking food, my cough goes unchecked due to smoke."

Another woman said. "Perhaps I have caught TB due to this."

A woman named Phoolmati said, "What should we do to take advantage of this scheme?"

Gaurav said, "Those of you who have got BPL card, all of

them should depositan application form duly filled in to the nearest LPG distribution centre. In this connection you will get other information from LPG distribution centre. Hearing it all women were overjoyed. They told one another, "We will go to our nearest LPG Distribution Centre tomorrow itself and getting free LPG connection will avail ourselves of the benefit of Ujjwala scheme."

Hearing their words Gaurav said with a smile, "Sure, sure, you must avail yourselves of this scheme. The government schemes are made so that the needy people may take advantage of them and the country may progress and prosper."

All women clapped to hear the words of Gaurav and in this way through Ujjwala scheme a wave of joy ran in the village.

❑

Sports Talent Search Portal

"Wah Kaushal, you play cricket very well. Where did you learn to play?" One day the class teacher madam Rima asked Kaushal.

"Madam, I have learnt playing on my own. My papa is very fond of watching cricket on TV and I also watched cricket along with him. Whereas papa concentrated on score and win of the Indian Cricket, my attention was pitched on the technique of the players and the pitch. Thus, I started playing with the street boys." The fourteen year old Kaushal told Rima.

Rima told it to the school Principal. Though there was no cricket team in the government school. The girls, no doubt, took part in football, Khokho etc. but Kaushal was interested only in cricket. The financial condition of her home was not good. Kaushal had twoyounger sisters. Father did whitewashing in homes and mother was a domestic help. In such a poor class the skill of Kaushal was displaying itself in the school.

Rima had taken special fancy to Kaushal. She wanted that her talent should not be confined to the school only, rather she should brighten the name of family and the society from her skill. Rima was the sports teacher. One day Rima was reading the newspaper. Suddenly she noticed that Prime Minister Narendra Modiji had launched National Sports Talent Search Portal, to bring to the fore the sports talent.

In this portal children above the age of eight can send their video. Rima was overjoyed to read this news. Immediately the figure of Kaushal emerged before her eyes. She told the Principal of her school about it.

Rima said, "The honourable Prime Minister Modiji has launched "National Sports Talent Search Portal" to carry talents like our Kaushal to the world level. It can be downloaded from Google Play and Apple Store on mobile phone and then demonstrating one's play that video can be uploaded there. By so doing if the Judges select it then she will not only get big opportunities to play but also to get golden training in it."

Principal said, "Rima, why delay then?" You make one or two videos of Kaushal and upload them on this portal. This will brighten the name of our school and a poor girl will get an opportunity to prove her talent."

After that Rima made two or three videos of Kaushal and uploaded them on National Sports Talent Search Portal".

Kaushal was very inquisitive. She wanted to know the result but so far there was no reply. Examinations started. Kaushal wrote her examination and then engaged herself in refining her play. One day Rima received a message that Kaushal plays cricket very well and so she has been selected to make her a great cricketer in the future. Getting this news Rima was beside herself with joy. When this news reached the parents of Kaushal, their eyes became moist out of joy. The mother and father of Kaushal embraced her and said, "Go, my daughter go, realize your dream and brighten the name of this country."

Thereafter, Kaushal set out on a new mission where the ball and batwere waiting for her.

In this way, National Sports Talent Search Portal filled in the hopes of Kaushal with new colour. ❑

One India, Great India

Today Mudit was very happy since morning. He was elected President of Delhi University. Mudit was very clever and promising. He was always in the fore front of other activities along with studies and he also had the capacity to lead. In his college most of the students had come from different states. They had their own language, dress and rituals. Modiji was to share his innermost thoughts with the countrymen on 11 September. He told the countrymen, "Different days are observed in colleges. Today is Rose Day, tomorrow same other day. Some people have antagonistic thoughts, but I am not an opponent to it. We have to promote creative talent and such talent is available in the university campus. Therefore we have to create feelings of unity and love in the University students. The country can progress only by doing this." At his words young people felt very happy. Thereafter Modiji said, "Have we ever thought that a college from Haryana observes Tamil Nadu Day, a college from Punjab observes Kerala Day? Dress like them, speak their language, eat rice from hand, play their games. In college students see Tamil films, read their literature in translation. By doing so the whole of India will be familiar with one another and understand one another's dress and food habits."

Mudit heard these things attentively. Having reached college he started applying these things. In the Delhi University he talked about organizing several competitions. Getting approval from the committee Mudit organized different languages competitions, all the same he motivated others to learn the work of Malayalam, Tamil, Gujarati and other languages. All students were happy to see such a function organized in Delhi University for the first time. Some students told Mudit, "After all, how did you think of affecting a confluence of Indian culture?"

Mudit replied with a smile, "Not I but the Prime Minister of our country honourable Narendra Modi had such a thought in his mind and just hearing them I decided to implement them. You know, "Where there is a will, there is a way." All we need is the courage to step up, the caravan is gathered all by itself as all of you liked this programme. Now such programmes will continue to go and our India will safely become great.

Other students endorsed the words of Mudit.

❑

Development of India

For a long time NRIs living in America were eager to see the Prime Minister of India. Among them A. K. Gill, Jasmin Desouza and Arti Ahuja were on high posts. The three knew each other very well. Reading news about Narendra Modi in the newspaper all the three were very excited. One day Arti said, "Gill, our country is really transforming. The kind of progress we are reading about and the way our children in games and other fields are earning glory for our country, give our mind utmost satisfaction."

"Absolutely Arti. Now our children are forging ahead even in education and are eager to show their talent in new fields"- Gill said.

Hearing the two Jasmine said, "Just a few days ago I come to know that Akash Manoj, a student of class X in a Tamil Nadu school has manufactured such an appliance through which one can find out the incoming "silent heart attack to a person and thus his life can be saved.

Hearing it Arti said, "Of course, most of the deaths in the world are caused by silent heart attack."

Just then Gill said, "The three children of Jaipur-Chaitanya, Mriganj Gujjar and Utsav Jain have made a startup company. That company has been granted feeding money of

3 crore rupees. That company manufactures health drinks. The special thing about this drink is that no preservative is used in it."

The three went on feeling glorified at the talent of those promising children. Just then they got the information that Prime Minister Narendra Modi was going to visit America in two days. Hearing it the three were thrilled like children and said, "Arre, we are going to miss this golden opportunity to see the Prime Minister."

In the programme several NRIs were present. Narendra Modi addressed them. In his speech he talked about issues right from the Surgical Strike to investment and economy. Narendra Modi was also excited to see the NRIs and particularly A. K. Gill, Jasmin and Arti were beside themselves with joy. They started talking about the good environment in India. Hearing it Narendra Modi met the NRIs with a smile and said, "Your heart must be ever asking you when our country would become like America. I assure you that it will happen in your life time. We will make it. There are 1.25 crore talented people in India and now they are getting congenial environment for it. We will very soon make a developed India. "At these words of the Prime Minister all NRIs applauded cheerfully. There was radiance on the faces of NRIs at that time and Gill, Jamin and Arti' were smiling to see each other. Arti said, "We should also make certain efforts so that we may help poor children living in India towards their education so that there is no obstruction in their education."

Gill said, "You have said the right thing, Arti. We NRIs together can institute a trust for the poor people. This scheme will definitely play a remarkable role in educating people." All agreed on this point and after Prime Minister left , they started talking with other NRIs about it. ❑

Electricity in Each Home

Pradanya was an intelligent student. She lived in such an area of Uttar Pradesh where there was absence of basic facilities like water, electricity and toilet. Her mausi (mother's sister) Paro was married in the Nander district of Maharashtra. Nander was much better compared to that area of Uttar Pradesh. One day, Paro came to live with her sister Ramo. During those days Pradanya was to be born. Paro had heard of this name in Nander. She had decided then and there to name her daughter 'Pradanya' but before that a daughter was born to Ramo and Paro herself named her Pradanya. True to her name Pradanya was very wise. When she was five years old her mother got her admitted to a government school. Her house had no electricity connection. Water, too, had to be brought from far off. Amid such inconvenience Pradanya was growing up. Whenever she went to her mausi's house she had a desire to study living there but to please her mother she had to come back.

Now she was in class X. She had a desire to become an engineer and bring in electricity in the house so that people did not have to suffer in the absence of electricity. Whenever Pradanya would go to mausi she would say, "Mausi, you will see, I will not accept defeat and in the most adverse circumstances facing all odds I will become an engineer. Then I will make available electricity to each home so that all homes have light and the country may progress."

Hearing her words Paro would embrace her and say, "My child, when there is a child like you, there is light already, no further light is needed."

At this Pradanya would burst out laughing.

In September 2007 on the occasion of Shivratri her school was closed. Whenever her school was closed, her favourite spot was Nander. Her parents were poor. In such a state how could they take their dear daughter out to visit places, so they would send her to Paro. There she took her books with her. Paro's husband Ramesh was a peon in a private firm. One day his boss gave his old computer to Ramesh. Ramesh knew a bit how to handle it. Whenever Pradanya was there he would teach her computer application. Now she had learnt to use the internet.

She had a television in her house. One day on 25thSeptember Pradanya was watching news with her mausi. Just then an important news flashed on the TV. "And now an important scheme announced by Prime Minister Modiji."

Just hearing it both Pradanya and Paro were all attention to know the details of the scheme. The news reader said, "Prime Minister Narendra Modi has started "Saubhagya" scheme on Monday to reach all homes electricity in both urban and rural areas."

Hearing it Pradanya's eyes opened wide out of joy and wonder. Paro noticed that there was joy and surprise on the face of Pradanya. The news reader further said, "Under Saubhagya scheme the target is to make electricity available in all villages, all towns by December 2018. Under this scheme the poor registered in the social, economic and ethnic census 2011 will be provided electricity free of charge. In difficult and remote areas those bereft of electricity, the Modi government will provide battery."

Now holding Paro, Pradanya started dancing. She did not hear what the newsreader said further. She had received the news most important to her. Though the newsreader went on to say, "In the free connection the poor people will be given a solar pack of 200 to 300 watt which will include 5 L.E.D. light, one DC fan, one DC power plug and five year maintenance." Turning off the TV Pradanya pointing to the newsreader said, "Now stop your nonsense." Let me enjoy now. Then she said to Paro, "Mausi, our Prime Minister has given to students such a big reward of life for whichthanking himmany times we will be insufficient. Now nobody can stop me from becoming the future engineer of the country. Now, in just a short time there will be electricity in my house."

Sharing Pradanya's joy Paro said, "Yes Pradanya, now you can live your life freely and you will not have to wait for the sun to read."

Hearing it Pradanya said, "Yes mausi, now the Prime Minister has provided for the night sun." Then both of them started laughing. Their laugh was the manifestation of lakhs –crores of Indians who were living dark lives in the absence of electricity.

❑

Respect the Teacher

This time Devans passed the interview for IAS. Though his rank was 117 but he was satisfied that in the third attempt he had made it. The day the letter of his success reached his home he was dancing with joy. Now he could marry Ina. Ina and Devans were classmates. Passing IAS last year Ina was the Deputy Director in the education department of Uttar Pradesh. He first wanted to inform Ina of it. Just then his mobile started ringing. It was Ina calling. Devans was amazed and thought to himself, "Perhaps the one we love, he/she already knows it in advance. Isn't it telepathy?" As he cheerfully called 'Hello', Ina said, "Congrats Dev. Now we are colleagues in profession as in college." Devans understood that Ina had seen his result on the internet. He said enthusiastically "Yea Ina. Now only our marriage remains to be."

Ina said, "On Saturday I am coming on a week's leave. This time you will give me a treat in a good restaurant."

After that Devans started waiting for Ina most eagerly. When Ina came, Devans kept staring at her. In a pink saree she was looking bewitchingly beautiful. Their two families gave their silent approval to their marriage. They reached a restaurant. People were trying there to listen to Modiji' "Man

Ki Baat' on the radio. On that Teacher's Day Modiji was to share his thoughts with people. To listen to Modiji all people were all attention in that restaurant. Ina said, "Dev, now we should also listen to such things carefully. They will prove very useful in our future career."

Dev said, "Yes Ina, you are right"

Just then 'Man ki Baat' started and Modiji's voice was heard, the other noises were heard no more.

Modiji said, "Whenever I would go to schools, I would often ask the teachers how many students they might have taught by then? Someone of them would say, he had taught 500 students, someone else said 700 students and still someone else said that he had taught almost 1000 students. Then I would ask, "Have they got married?" The teacher would say, "Some of them may have got married". Again I would ask them, "How many students invited you to their marriage?" Hearing it all were stunned. Only one or two students had invited their teachers to their marriage. It means that after getting education students are totally cut off from their teachers. The role of teachers should never go off from our life. On auspicious occasions of their life students should invite their teachers first, friends and others afterward. Brothers and sisters, teachers are the pillars of students. On their foundation itself the strong edifice of students is elected. As a result of their teaching, affection and chastisement they are able to reach their target. So, they must be treated with utmost respect."

Hearing it Ina and Devans looked at each other and were lost in their old memories. At school Ina and Devans were in the same class. There was always a competition between them to stand first and Ina won every time. Yes, if Devans stood first it was with Ina together. Ina never let Devans stand first alone. Shashi ma'am who taught them Science always encouraged both Ina and Devans. She was always with them. Had there been no guidance of Shashi ma'am perhaps they wouldnot have cleared IAS because in that age both of them were attracted to each other. Shashi ma'am had understood it and advised them separately that they should first mind their career and when they are successful though belonging to different castes their families would easily accept them. Both of them had realized it. That's why today they were at the successful end of their career.

Recalling that period and getting emotional Ina said, "Dev, let's go to school tomorrow itself. There we will meet Shashi ma'am and apprise them of our success and also invite her to our marriage."

Dev replied smilingly, "Yea Ina! Done. It'll be a nice feeling to go to our school after such a long period." A few minutes later both of them set out to buy a good gift and sweets for Shashimaa'm . After all, the news of two happy events is not conveyed empty handed.

❑

Skill Development & Training

"Naresh, what happened? The result of XII has come out today. Your result also must have come. Have you failed this time, too?" Gautam asked.

"Yes friend! Schooling is beyond my reach. I don't understand anything. I don't dare to go home today. It is my third year in XII. My parents were having a great expectation. What will happen now? You know that economically we are not very sound. In this situation my parents' concern is genuine. I don't know what to do."

"It does not matter. You need not be disappointed. Haven't heard about Prime Minister Skill Development Programme? It was launched particularly for youth like you in 2015."

"OK. Is it so! Tell me about it. I don't know much about this."

"Listen to me carefully. This scheme aims at developing skills for those students who have left their education after X or XII. At the same time there are also young men who have some skill but don't have a certificate. Nowadays, it is necessary to have a certificate for employment. Not only this Naresh, those who get training under Skill Development Programme given awards also. Its certificates are valid all over India."

"OK. Gautam, tell me what are the illegibility criteria for admission in this programme?"

"Oh friend! I told you this programme is particularly meant for those youth who do not have higher education. He must be a citizen of India. Online application form is to be filled in for this. I will get it done. Tell me about the course you want to apply for."

"Well, tell me the name of the courses."

"There are so many courses in it. I will show you the complete list of the courses on computer. It includes courses like agriculture, manufacturing, plumbing and construction, electronics, handicrafts, healthcare, green job, logistics, life science, tourism, textile and handlooms, etc. In Prime Minister Skill Development Programmes youths will be trained keeping in mind the programmes like Make in India, National Solar Mission, Clean India, Digital India run by the central government so that trained persons can create jobs for themselves and add the other unemployed young men to them."

"Well, the most important thing is to know their fee." Naresh asked.

"Very good question. Countless young men do not get admission in private training institutes because their fees are too high for the lower class people. Keeping these things in mind all courses under Prime Minister Skill Development Programme are made free of cost. Deserving and lower class people will be specially benefited from it. The government has allocated a rich fund for this programme, under which twenty four lakh youths will be trained in the first year. By the end of the year, 2022 the target is to take this figure to around forty crore. Those who pursue these courses with diligence, will be able to launch their own enterprises and take them to greater heights in the future. A good thing about these courses is that their duration ranges from three months to six months and to maximum one year. In this way you will be able to earn and support your father within a short period of time."

" Gautam, you are the friend in need. You have solved my problem. Till then, I have been thinking what will I say to my parents. But the Prime Minister Skill Development Programmes have restored my lost confidence. Please give me all relevant information about Prime Minister Skill Development Programmes, tomorrow. I will seriously pursue the course. Tomorrow I will select the course of my choice after going through the list of courses. Now I am going home; my parents would be waiting there."

"Yes, Naresh, go home and tell your parents that you are not unsuccessful but, you are going to take a new step towards success. You need their blessings in this new venture."

Having said this Naresh hugged Gautam and left for home with a new determination in his eyes.

❑

Statues of Great Men

Anshika was the President of the students union of her college. She took great care to ensure that proper facilities are made available to all students. One day students of the college said to Anshika, "Examinations in the college are going to start shortly. Thereafter, we will part our ways. Why don't we organise a picnic at some beautiful spot to make it a memorable moment."

The Secretary, Ayushi, also agreed to this proposal. Thereafter, in a short time a beautiful picnic spot was selected. Anshika said to all students, "We will all go to picnic, but all of you have to bring some cooked food."

All students gave their consent.

Aditya said, "I will bring puri. My mom makes very good puri."

Ilisha responded to him, "Aditya, I will eat puris, but you have to cook them. Bhai, I will eat puris cooked only by you."

At this Aditya replied, "Yes, I will make them myself. I am of modern world. I do not think that domestic chores are meant only for girls."

Then Yashaswi said winking at him, "Aditya, what's the matter? You have completely impressed Ilisha. You seem a little more influenced by the movie "Kee And Ka." Everyone burst into laughter at this. Anshika said smilingly while making them silent, “No personal comment. Come on. You should decide among yourselves what each one of you will bring. I have to attend to so many activities.” Saying this Anshika and Ayushi proceeded to look after other activities of the college. In the class room Ilisha, Aditya, Yashaswi, Medha, Sanyam, Aarush and Agastya excitedly got engaged in making the list of things each one of them will bring.

Next day they all turned up in their favourite dresses well prepared with the requisite items. Anshika had arranged a bus. They were forty studentsaltogether. They all reached the picnic spot laughing and playing antarakshari. It was named Sadabahar Lake (Evergreen Lake). There was a beautiful lake there and there was a statue of Sardar Vallabhbhai Patel along with Gandhiji. There were some more statues of revolutionary leaders. Besides these trees of maulsiri, gudahal, amaltas etc in abundance were adding to the beauty of its ambience. All students enjoyed themselves thoroughly. Thereafter, they opened their lunch-boxes and had lunch together. After lunch they got busy chatting among themselves. In the meanwhile, Anshika's attention was drawn to the lake and the statues of the great men and it flushed her face. She rushed to the students and said, 'Who will say that we are educated? Have a glance at the lake. Our food remains, paper, etc. are littered around. When we came here; it was a beautiful sight, and now only litters are seen around here. Look at the statues of our great men who had worked tirelessly to make India beautiful. How much dust coated they are! Was it not our duty to pay obeisance to these great men and clean their statues before having fun and all that? Oof!I got upset to see your such activities. Yesterday, itself the Prime Minister in his 'Man ki

Baat' questioned, can't we imbibe it in our normal habit to look after the statues of those great men; we are emotional about installing their statues. Why can't we make cleanliness along with the practice of cleaning the statues of great men without the government aid a part of our life? Tell me. Just now we were talking about our rights that we want this and that, too; but we are indifferent to our duties. Why? Tell me.

No one had any answer. They realised their mistake. Seeing everyone silent, Anshika said, "The way we enjoyed at the picnic spot; with the same spirit we will clean this place and wash off the dust from these statues to make them shine. On hearing Anshika's words they got up and started cleaning the place. They cleaned the whole place within a short time. At the same time Aditya, Ilisha, Sanyam and Aarush began cleaning the statues.

In a short time statues of great men along with Sadabahar Lake were smiling like the evergreen lake as if they were blessing the students that the reign of sanitation, health, and development lies in their hands. That's why they should do their work with determination and keep public places clean.

The Prime Minister Modiji's appeal was proving successful through these students.

❑

Construction of Toilet

Raman was married to Pradeep. They did not have much education. Pradeep worked in a private firm. Raman was not highly educated but was very intelligent. She was married at Patowapura in Madhya Pradesh. When she was young her friends used to tease her that her name was like a boy's. Raman answered back, "What is there in name? Our work makes all the difference. We should do such work that makes the people forget the differences between boys and girls."

On the very next day of the marriage she saw that the ladies of the house were asking her to go out with them. Raman asked surprisingly, "Where are we to go so early in the morning?" Her jethani (elder sister-in-law) Devaki said, "For toilet. It will be difficult to get a place after sunrise." On hearing it Raman was astonished. She said, "Isn't there a toilet in the house?"

She burst into tears and grew miserable. She told her husband, "I can't live for a minute in a house where there is no toilet."

Pradeep replied, "Right now, toilet is not available in any house here. When we have money, we will have toilets, too."

But Raman did not go out with other women of the house for toilet. Somehow she spent two- three days wailing in the house.

Raman was fond of listening to radio. Her father had gifted her a good quality radio at the time of her marriage farewell. It was Sunday and the programme 'Man ki Baat' was to be broadcast on radio. Raman switched on the radio at high volume. Incidentally Modiji was speaking on Open Defecation on that day. He said, "In order to make Clean India Movement successful, we will have to ensure construction of toilets, awareness for the use of toilet, proper solid and liquid waste management, we have to promote the habit of washing hands with soap and impose penalty against those who litter." Then while referring to Seema Patel of Baitul in Madhya Pradesh he added, "Newly wedded bride Seema Patel had left her father-in-law's house because it did not have a toilet. The news spread in the whole gram panchayat. The gram panchayat not only got a toilet built there but also brought the bride Seema Patel back with a band playing on musical instruments."

All those who were listening to radio with Raman heard this message. Pradeep decided to get a toilet built in the house earliest possible by any means and to make Modiji's mission of 'Clean India' a success.

He said to Raman, "Today, you have opened my eyes. Till date we all used to think it unnecessary to have a toilet in the house. But today, you and Prime Minister Modiji's talks opened my eyes. I promise to get a toilet built in the house within a fortnight."

On hearing the words of Pradeep, Raman got excited and said, "That's like a good husband. He should contribute to keep his country along with the home clean and beautiful.

When the toilet is built in our house, I will motivate other women of the village for toilets."

Pradeep responded to her compliments, "It is usually said that the gate of a wife's fortune opens when she gets a good husband. But I would say that my fortune took a favourable turn on getting a good and prudent wife."

Raman smiled on hearing his complimentary words and got into her domestic chores.

❑

Save Electricity

Damini was preparing for Civil Services. She was very intelligent. Everyone was impressed with her personality and intelligence. Everyone acceded to her because of her mental skill, cleverness and talent. She was pursuing her MA from Delhi University besides preparing for Civil Services. A few days ago, she heard the Prime Minister Modiji declaring that under 'Sobhagya Yojana' every village, every town will get electricity by December 2018 so that everyone can lead a happy life with basic rights and amenities. Damini was a responsible citizen. Anyway, she was a future IAS. One day her younger sister Piya came to her and said, "Didi (elder sister), I have to make a model on the subject—'Save Electricity'. Besides making the model, I have to write my opinion also. Please help me."

Damini responded to Piya, "I will certainly help you." Thereafter, she began turning over books. Suddenly she chanced upon a book named "Modi Prabandhan". In that book, Modiji had narrated his thoughts about electricity. At one place she read that Modiji advised some local residents that on a full moon night they should come out after switching off all lights in their homes and street lights. In this way when everyone assemble outside, it will take shape of a fair. People will understand one another, and talk among themselves. This is how all Indians will get united and at the same time it will save electricity. Not only this, a competition of inserting thread into the eye of the needle in the moon light can be organised. Damini went on reading that book and the model for Piya got ready in her mind. She not only helped Piya in making her model but also told her how to make a presentation of the model. Piya's model stood first not only in her school but in all schools of the district. Having seen this Damini decided that Piya's model will not be kept just as a model, but will be implemented on the ground. The night of Purnima (full moon) was at hand. The clear view of full moon was expected in that night. She went to every home in her neighbourhood and requested them to come out at 8 p.m after switching off all lights in their homes. She has to show them something. Damini was a talented student and dear to all in the colony. On the full moon night most of her neighbourhood quickly completed their domestic work, switched off all lights and assembled in the park of the colony. Damini was there with needles and thread.

When everyone gathered there an old man said, "Damini Bitiya (daughter), you were to show us some strange and unique thing. Show us."

Damini replied with a smile, "Uncle, this is the unique thing that you are watching. We all are busy in our world. One does not know one's neighbours. How pleasant we feel in this park, today! There is hustle and bustle and the moon in the sky is at her best. Henceforth, we will meet at this park on every Purnima, talk among ourselves, will share each other views. Not only this, we will play games also. People should never give up their childhood. Childhood is the symbol of energy and enthusiasm in a man."

They all agreed to Damini and said, "Really we are feeling very well here today and getting peace in this cool night of Damini." After this Damini organized a 'needle and thread' competition among Piya and some other young people an really it turned into a fair like situation. Everywhere the rain of laughter and the feeling of gaiety, love and cordiality was visible.

When the contest was over, Damini said, "Our Prime Minister has pledged to take electricity to every village by 2018. In order to realise that resolve we all, every Indian should cooperate with him. By switching off all lights in our homes on every Purnima we will not only support our country but also share and care one another."

On hearing these words of Damini, all neighbours along with her parents were feeling proud of her and even the moon was shining brighter to see Damini's intelligence as if she was spreading her smile with her sharp brightness.

❑

India Reads

Prashansa was fond of reading books since her childhood. When she was studying in school, the library period was on every Tuesday. She used to finish the book she borrowed from the library on Tuesday itself. And by the next Tuesday she used to go through all the books issued to the students of the class. Everyone was familiar with her love for books. The students of her class had given her different names. Some called her 'Phadaku' (voracious reader), others called 'bibliophile', while some others addressed her as 'walking library'. Gradually Prashansa crossed the steps of the school. She became an editor in a government office and writer as well. Many of her books sold in the market like hot cakes. One day Prashansa was assigned to prepare a project on Gujarat. While collecting information and data about Gujarat, she learnt about the movement 'Baanche Gujarat'. This movement was launched by the then Chief Minister of Gujarat Sri Narendra Modiji so that more and more people should get connected with the libraries and read books. Reading new books helps in physical and mental growth of an individual; and he walks in tandem with the country with full awareness.Just by reading this, Prashansa got an idea of extending the movement 'Baanche Gujarat' to 'Baanche

India'. She herself had so many books at her home. She collected all those books. She took along with her some more students who were ready to volunteer for this work. In this way she soon got a vacant space where books could be kept. The students associated with her knocked at every door and invited people from young to old to visit the library started in the colony whenever they had time. Inspired by this initiative of Prashansa many people came forward to extend all possible help. Some subscribed to the Newspapers for the library, while some payed for magazines. It was named 'Apani Library' (Own Library). It welcomed everyone who was interested in acquiring knowledge. The library shot into fame shortly. It motivated many people to read new books and at the same time it developed their knowledge.

If everyone like Prashansa comes forward in this way to take initiative to motivate people for reading books, the dream of the Prime Minister will certainly be realised soon and India will become a fully literate country.

❑

The Courage of Manpreet

Manpreet was living with her family at Karnal. In her district the number of daughter was very poor. The Prime Minister announced a movement 'Beti Bachao, Beti Padhao' (Save daughter, Teach daughter) on 22nd January 2014. Manpreet listened to it very attentively. In the meantime, 161 such districts from the country were selected where the ratio of daughter was less than sons. Karnal was one of them. Manpreet felt very sorry to hear it and resolved to improve the girl child ratio. She had the aptitude for social service since her childhood and used to help the needy from time to time.

She was an English teacher in a government school. She had two young daughters tender like a flower.--Amanpreet and Namanpreet. They were twins. So her husband Pritam Singh at times said, "Manno, there must be a son."

Manpreet replied, "Sorry, I do not agree with you at all. We have to ensure good future for our children. Anyway, since when I learnt that our district is one of those where the number of daughters is too less than that of sons, I felt very sad. We will look after our daughters properly and give them the best possible education. Nowadays daughters are superior to sons. The daughters of India are in headlines right from Saniya Mirza to Saina Nehwal, from Geeta Phogat to Babita Phogat. Therefore, you will never speak before me that there should have been a son."On hearing her words Preetam Singh said, "OK, my mother, I will not say. To tell you the truth, I am proud to have a lady like you as my wife. You are excellent in every work from domestic chores to field work. Even in rendering help to others you are ahead of everyone."

"Hold, hold, do not praise too much. Pay attention to my words. Right from today for a few hours a day we will move from house to house and campaign for 'Beti Bachao, Beti Padhao'. Government is doing its work, but along with that, it is also our duty to work in tandem with programmes launched for the development of the country." Pritam Singh agreed to her. Thereafter, it became their daily routine. After coming back from school, Manpreet completed her domestic work, taught her daughters and in the evening both husband and wife used to go to village Chaupal, assemble the villagers and tell them that daughters are at the top everywhere. If the number of daughters in our district continued going down, the young men will have to remain unmarried and several other problems will emerge in the country."

It is not that the people received the couple with all honour. Many people used to make gossips about Manpreet and pass pinching comments on her. But Manpreet was well determined to make Modiji's mission a success. In association with her husband Pritam Singh, she braved all obstacles and crossing all hurdles she kept on marching to success. Her striving bore fruit and people not only started showing reverence to Manpreet but also paid attention to her words and followed her. In this way within two and a half years

Karnal showed improvement and the number of daughters started going up.

All this happened because of Manpreet's rigorous struggle. Now she was very happy because at her place everyone came to understand that daughters are precious like diamonds and can achieve any goal with their courage and diligence.

❑

Top University

Aadil, Pankul, Prarthana, Iccha and Sameer—all five were studying in Patna University. They were very good friends. They all were highly talented one better than another. Aadil was very good at writing, and was doing MA in Hindi. Pankul loved Physics. He was pursuing BA Honours in Physics. His aim was to become a scientist. Prarthana was fond of Maths and Chemistry. Prarthana puzzled everyone by solving the sums of Mathematics from new methods. Everyone felt that one day Prarthana will certainly bag Nobel Prize in Mathematics. She was highly influenced by the Mathematician Sriniwas Ramanujam. She regarded him her ideal in the field of Mathematics.

One day Adil told her while teasing, "Friend, Srinivas Ramanujam left this world at an early age of 33. But within this short period he left an indelible mark on the world with his startling revelations in Mathematics. Had he lived for some long period, he would have certainly got the Nobel Prize. It seems he has taken rebirth in the shape of Prarthana and will not stop till she gets Nobel Prize." Prarthana responded to it, "All right, I will get the Nobel Prize in Mathematics and you will get the same in Hindi. Till date there is a vacancy for the Nobel Prize in Hindi Literature."

Pankul, Iccha, and Sameer used to smile at such talks. Iccha was a good orator and Sameer had leadership quality. Once they were talking among themselves. Pankul said, "I think that I should go abroad after doing B.Sc. in Physics. Talent does not get recognition here. Anyway, we don't have a world class university in India."

Iccha reacted to it, "Pankul, a university cannot become a world class on its own. Along with the government, we all have to work for this." In the meanwhile, it was announced in the college that honourable Prime Minister Narendra Modi will be inaugurating the centenary celebration of Patna University on 14 October, 2017. They were overjoyed. Prarthana said, "You will see, the Prime Minister will definitely make some announcement that will be good for us."

Sameer added, "I, too, feel so." And then turning to Pankul he said, "Then talented students like you will not have to go abroad for research and study. All facilities will be easily available here."

On 14 October, 2017 the University was well decorated for the reception of the Hon'ble Prime Minister. Students were agog with excitement. After the inaugural function when Modiji rose to address, everyone sat attentively listening with curiosity to what he said. Modiji said, "Top twenty universities of the country will be developed as world class. It will consist of ten private and ten government universities. These universities will get autonomy. And the Central Government will provide ten thousand crore in the next five years." It drew huge applause from the audience with the slogan 'Modi-Modi' renting the sky. Prarthana, Pankul, Iccha, Aadil and Sameer jumped from their seats in joy. Modiji said, "I would like to take Patna University one step forward. There is not a single university of India in the list of top 500 universities. The fund of rupees ten thousand crore would be disbursed among ten government and ten private universities. There will be a competition among all the universities applying for the grant. Only the universities which get through this competition will get the fund. The attempt will be made to develop them as world standard universities with the help of this fund. By 2022 we have to make Bihar a developed state."

On hearing it Prarthana and Iccha hugged each other and said, "Hurrah! Really the words of the Prime Minister pleased us. Now there will be a greater unfolding of our talent. All the students will strive to take their respective universities to the top and in this way with the collective effort of the students and the government India, too, will have top universities."

All students welcomed the words of the Prime Minister with applause. After the end of the programme, Prarthana, Pankul, Iccha, Aadil and Sameer sat in the canteen and began chalking out plans for their future and for taking the university to the top.

❑

Country of Snakes

It is about that time when Narendra Modiji was learning tricks of politics. Once he went to Taiwan for some assignment of the party. He did not know the language of Taiwan. To get rid of this problem an interpreter was assigned to him. Modiji spoke in English and the interpreter interpreted the same in the native language to his audience. The interpreter used to spend a lot of time with him because he was the only means to communicate with the gentry of the country. Modiji's ideas and thoughts reached the leaders of Taiwan through him. In leisure period Modiji used to talk to him informally. The interpreter used to ask him about India. One day he asked Modiji, "India is a very big country in respect of civilisation and culture. The culture of India is an imitable example for all countries in the world. Despite being so many good things in India there is something that dents the image of India."

Modiji responded to his query, "No, it's not so. How did you think so? Tell me,may be, I can clear your doubt."

The interpreter said, "Earlier India used to be called a country of snakes and snake-charmers. It is believed that the people are illiterate there, and being trapped in the whirlpool of illiteracy they believe in snakes and snake-charmers and superstitions. Indians are bound to their paupered traditions and they can lay their life for them."

The interpreter told the truth. But Modiji replied cheerfully, "It happened in those days, when the rate of illiteracy was high in India. But with the passage of time the rate of literacy has rapidly increased. Indians are very intelligent. India gave to the world great scientists like Aryabhatta and Jagdish Chandra Basu. Besides the different cultural attires, cuisines, and festivals, India gave to the world the concept of zero. If you visit India some time now, you will find the country playing with mouse. Indian technology is at its height now. You will see that shortly many of the policies of our country will have their colours on the whole world and give a new identity to the country."

The interpreter responded to Modiji, "Sir, if the country has a striving, diligent and laborious personality like you, its every policy and style will certainly be spectacular."

Today after being the Prime Minister of India Narendra Modiji has certainly left an indelible mark on the whole world with the use of technology and strategy.

❑

Ayurvedic Hospital

Vikas was very happy today. He had done B. Sc. in agriculture. He was engaged in agriculture at Gulawati. He was dear to all villagers. After all why not; he was the only educated, clear minded young farmer who walked with the time. Vikas used to visit Indian Agricultural Research Institute, New Delhi from time to time and learn about new crops and new varieties of crops. He had bumper crops of paddy and wheat in his fields. When wheat crop in his fields bloomed, the old farmers said, "Bhai, the wheat crop of Vikas had really the glaze of gold." On 17 October, 1017, the day of Dhanteras (a festival celebrated a day before Diwali) the Prime Minister, Narendra Modi inaugurated the first All India Institute of Ayurveda at New Delhi. Vikas often listened to radio in his fields. He used to listen to radio programmes like 'Gunje Swar Ganw ke' (Echo the Voice of Village), 'Gram Sansar' (World of Village), and 'Krishi Jagat' (Agro world). His general knowledge was far better than that of other peasants. He was hearing the repeated announcement in news since today morning that the Prime Minister has inaugurated an All India Institute of Ayurveda at New Delhi. He listened to the news related to it in detail.

In the evening, elderly villagers were sitting at the

chaupal and considering the next day's programme. The oldest peasant Ramvir said, "It is Small Diwali tomorrow. But the real Diwali of the peasants comes when crops in our fields bloom. Many a time our crops are wasted because of drought or rough weather. At that time several difficulties come up."

Before Ramvir could add further, Vikas said, "Baba, now it is not so. You know, there are some shortcomings on our side, also. We keep treading on the centuries old traditions. We do not try to change according to time and need. The Prime Minister of our country Modiji said today itself that along with the conventional farming peasants' unused land should be used for growing medicinal plants. I.T revolution that is a revolution pertaining to computer and machine that has taken place in our country in the last thirty years and now health revolution should come up. Baba Ramdev and other renowned names in Ayurveda have such knowledge that can give us remedy for great diseases. With this, young farmers like us should take its benefit and cultivate medicinal plants in the unused land after getting information from you.

On hearing it eighty year old Tota Ram said, "Son, what an idea! Anyway, it is the anniversary of Dhanwantri. Dhanwantri himself did not consider anything a better alternative to Ayurved and herbal plants for treatment. However, medical treatment of today was not available in those days."

Vikas said, "Exactly, grandpapa. Today Modiji also said that our players keep physiotherapists in sports. Ayurvedic therapy can also play an important role in the field of sports. Not only this, Ayurveda can also be effective in keeping armed forces mentally focused and stress free. Today Modiji also talked about establishing Ayurvedic hospital at different places. Now the government is doing this much. So how can development take place if we, the common people do not work hand to hand with him?"

Chandrabhan uncle who was sitting there smilingly said, "Bhai, you have rightly said. As long as Gulawati does not join hands with Vikas, it cannot develop."

At this everyone smiled. Vikas also smiled because he had understood that all old men present there were in agreement with him; and they were now ready to focus on modernisation and new technology in place of conventional means in the field of agriculture. Vikas said, "Uncle, I am not only with my village, but with the whole country and if every young man like me moves forward with this thought, take it for granted, every day in our country will be Diwali and we will celebrate every day." Everyone agreed to Vikas and blessed him, and said that they would ask their grandchildren to take inspiration from Vikas.

Now, night had approached. Today, on the day of Dhanteras a row of some earthen lamps appeared before the houses of the village. The flames of those lamps, as it were, were ready to tell every visitor that their village is changing now and marching on the path of development.

❑

Diwali of Soldiers

Major Alok was back home. He was posted at a Cantonment area in Rajasthan. He belonged to Dogra Regiment. Balbir Kaur, the mother of Major Alok was very happy to see her son at home in Diwali. She was engaged in making Rangoli and at the same time talking to him. All of a sudden her eyes got moist. On seeing her eyes moist, Major Alok said, "What happened Maa? Why are tears in your eyes on the festival of Deepawali?

Balbir Kaur said, "Son, had your father Colonel Saheb been alive today, the pleasure of this festival would have been doubled."

On hearing his mother's words, Major Alok's eyes also suddenly turned tearful. He said, "Maa, father had sacrificed his life for the security of his country; and I am very much proud of my father. Like him I will also be always ready to lay my life."

Balbir Kaur said while wiping her tears, "Son, everyone should serve his country. But at times I feel that those who lay their life for their motherland are made to suffer its ill consequences. It does not make much difference to the common man or to the government."

At this, Major Alok reacted, "No mother, you are saying this out of your self-interest. It is not so at all. Those who achieve martyrdom on the border of the country make difference to the heart of every Indian and the government, too. You know that the Prime Minister came to celebrate Diwali with us at the Dogra War Memorial in 2015. Not only this, our Prime Minister Narendra Modiji celebrates Diwali with the forces on the border every year since he became the Prime Minister. In 2014 when the soldiers were engaged in defending their motherland while shivering in cold at Siachen, the Prime Minister suddenly reached there and created a warm atmosphere even in the snow. Every soldier felt honoured to find the Prime Minister among themselves. In 2016 he celebrated the same with the forces of Indo-Tibet Border Police at Kinnor Indo-China border in Himachal Pradesh; and on this Diwali he has reached Gurej Sector situated at the L O C in Jammu & Kashmir. Now, you tell me, when the Prime Minister of the country, taking into account their hard work and struggle of the armed forces, celebrates the festival of light with them, what else do you want? The snow of Siachen melts down to see the passion and enthusiasm of the Prime Minister and a smile flickers on the face of every soldier. In this, every Indian eats sweets with the Prime Minister on Diwali, embraces one another and takes pledge that he will be forever committed to the safety of Mother India." Saying this tears dropped from Major Alok's eyes.

At this Balbir Kaur said, "I was wrong, son. You are right. On this festival of Alok (light), my house is full of light. This Alok (light) is only lighting my home but also making a significant contribution in lighting every home of the country."

After this Balbir Kaur along with Alok began the rituals of Diwali. At that time it was not only Major Alok's house that was glittering with lights but the whole country was adorned with the radiance of Alok. □

Leader of Twitter

Narendra Modiji is one of those leaders who believe in marching along with time. He takes very little rest and most of the time he is striving to take the country to the path of development. Modiji keeps visiting various countries in order to take India to global standards. In course of it he holds discussions with the foreign leaders and in cooperation with them he makes plans with which India and other countries can work together for a better future. In this course once he met the President of Russia, Vladimir Putin. A number of foreign news reporters had been there. Many reporters were anxious to have a glimpse of Narendra Modiji. Incidentally at that time Megyn Kelly, the anchor of National Broadcasting Company was also present there. She is very popular for her presentation of the programme. Megyn Kelly kept on asking several questions from both the leaders. Suddenly she turned to the Prime Minister, Modi and said, "Does P M Modi use Twitter?"

People present there were stunned at the question of world-fame anchor, Megyn Kelly and wondered if Megyn Kelly had come without doing homework about the Prime Minister Narendra Modi. But the Prime Minister Modi answered Megyn Kelly unaffectedly with a smile, "Yes, I am on twitter."

After this when Megyn Kelly met other reporters, a reporter asked, “Kelly, you have earned so much reputation for your presentation. Then how did you commit such a blunder today?”

In response to her fellow reporter's question, she said, “What mistake? What did I do?”

Another reporter replied, “Dear Kelly, don't you know that Indian Prime Minister Narendra Modi has 30 million followers on twitter and 41 million followers on his Facebook?”

Megyn Kelly was aghast to hear it. Then a reporter said, “Kelly, not only this, Narendra Modiji is the second most followed leader on twitter. The President of America, Donald Trump is in the first place.” Kelly was stunned to hear it. Now she looked at the Prime Minister Modiji who was busy discussing with other Ministers after giving answer to Kelly's nonsensical question in a normal way.

❑

My Government

"Asha, you have done a wonder. You have passed XII examination with 93 percent marks. You want to be an administrative officer. It seems to me that your road to become an IAS is clear now."

Asha's face faded on hearing Vineeta's words. She said, "Vinita, now I will have to go away from my parents to get admission in a college. I know that my parents cared so muchto give me a good education. They also sent me to a faraway school. If there was a good college in my area, I would study there living with my parents."

At this Vineeta said, "You are rightly saying this. It does not matter. It is necessary for you to go out from here to get good education", Asha said while brooding over something, "I think, I should write a letter to the Prime Minister expressing my view that it is necessary to open good colleges everywhere to increase percentage of education. So that talented students need not go away for getting education."

In the meanwhile, Hindi teacher Pratibha Chawala entered there. She said, "Congratulations Asha! You have brought laurels to our school. Don't you know that the government has launched a platform named "My Government" to share your opinions and suggestions?"

Hearing it, Asha said while scratching her head, "Yes Madam, I know it. But please tell me about it in detail."

Pratibha patted her head lovingly and said, "Come, sit down. I will tell you at ease."

Thereafter, both Asha and Vineeta sat down at the desk. Pratibha began, "Prime Minister Modi launched "My Government" platform on the completion of the sixty days of his government on 26 July, 2014. This platform empowers the citizens of India to contribute to the good governance."

Vineeta said, "Wonderful! It is a very good platform."

Pratibha added, "While launching this platform Modiji said that the success of democracy is impossible without participation of people. So many people want to contribute to nation- building and invest their time and energy. They only need the opportunity to contribute and show their contribution."

At this Vineeta said looking at Asha, "Asha, now you should definitely share your opinions and suggestions on this platform."

Pratibha Madam said, "My Government portal offers several opportunities to those who want to move ahead from exchange of ideas on this portal to work on the ground. Any citizen can send his or her entry for this."

Asha said, "Its application and management will be very difficult."

Pratibha madam replied, "National Informatics Centre (NIC) and Electronics and Information Technology Department implement and manage 'My Government" portal and it helps in getting the participation of citizens in good governance. 'Group' and 'Corner' are important parts of "My Government". This portal is divided into groups like 'Clean Ganga', 'Girls Education', 'Clean India', 'Skill India' and 'Employment Creation'. Every group is assigned online and on ground jobs which will be accomplished by the contributors. Not only this, the portal has achieved promising results. Lakhs of suggestions have come to the portal MyGov since 2014 and 300 to 400 out of it are very significant. Some of these suggestions have been implemented and some are in the process. You know that nowhere in the world the government has sought the opinion of the common man on such a wide scale on policy making."

Asha said, "Madam, it is really a very good platform through which common men are able to send their opinions direct to the Prime Minister. With this portal the Prime Minister has linked the people directly with the development."

Pratibha madam smilingly said, "Absolutely correct, Asha. With this MyGov portal has given new hope to many Ashas (Hopes) like you; through which talented students like you can directly join hands with the government and make their meaningful contribution."

"You have rightly said, Madam. I will do so. When the Prime Minister has given an open platform for development to every citizen; it becomes our responsibility to contribute to it."

On hearing it Pratibha smilingly said, "Well done Asha! I hope you will make our school and the country proud."

Thereafter, the bell rang and Pratibha ma'am left for her next class.

❑

Young Entrepreneur

"Viral, you are really a source of inspiration for young men. In my opinion, you should meet our Chief Minister Modiji. He feels pleased to see young men like you rising."

"Prafulla, it is the words and deeds of Modiji that motivate and encourage me to do something. Not only I but every young man according to his/her capacity must do something that helps the country develop."

"Absolutely, Viral. You rightly said. Now, you see yourself. Besides doing B Com., MBA and MA, you are the owner of a cloth processing unit and are doing social-service as well. You have nothing to do with politics. Besides running your cloth processing unit you are doing commendable job of protecting environment and creating energy with full commitment. What's your age—just, 31? You have still miles to go."

After a long chat, Prafulla went away from there and Viral smilingly got into his work. Whoever meets Viral once cannot but be impressed with his talent and achievements at this young age. Once an official appointed in the Department of Industry at Surat came to know about Viral. When he came to know about Viral's achievements, he was deeply influenced by him. He said, "In my opinion, you should submit your application for the highest award for quality in Environment Protection and State MAMI (Micro, Medium and Small scale Industry) of Gujarat."

Viral sent his application and incidentally he won that award, too. Viral was invited to Vibrant Gujarat Summit held at Gandhinagar to receive this award. There, Narendra Modiji himself was giving away awards to the winners. When Viral went to the stage to receive the award, Modiji said in surprise looking at Viral, "Have you really won this award? You are looking so young."

Viral smilingly said to Modiji, "Yes sir, I have won this award." Modiji said while congratulating him, "The country is proud of young men like you; and the country really needs young men like you."

These words of Modiji, as if, gave wings to his dreams. Henceforth, Viral, leaving behind well-known companies, bagged Environment Award at a national level.

Viral has also organised Cancer Medical Camp for tribal women; and he calls Modiji as the source of inspiration for all this. He says that a new age will dawn in India shortly where India will be highly developed and every young man will be steadfast and educated.

❑

Gifts from a Volunteer

Kanchan Banerjee was very happy, today. He came to know that the RSS volunteer and Chief Minister of Gujarat is coming to Boston to meet immigrant Indians. Kanchan decorated his home and kept waiting for the Chief Minister of Gujarat. When his dream came true, his happiness knew no bounds. He along with his full family welcomed Modiji. Modiji greeted them with a smile and warmly said, "I feel very happy to see the Indians prospering."

Rounds of food and drink continued. Kanchan had bought for Modiji many gifts of her choice. She offered all those gifts to him and said, "Sir, when you go back to India, you will carry with you some of our sweet memories. These worthless gifts are for you."

Looking at the gifts Modiji said, "I am a Pracharak (Missionary) and I cannot accept gifts from anybody. I called on you, talked to you, heard something about India from you and shared with you something of my own. That's all. What else can be more special!"

Kanchan insisted, "No, you have to take along something from here. The culture of India tells that one should never be sent back from home empty handed."

At this Modiji replied, "Kanchanji, you are creating an

emotional situation by dragging Indian culture in it. But even then I will not accept the gift."

Kanchan added, "Sir, don't take any gift. Please accept a little present for souvenir, so that it reminds you and India of us."

When Kanchanji refused to give in by any means, Modiji had a look at her room. A laptop was lying there. Modiji said, "If you are so desirous, you give this modern laptop. I will easily acquire technical knowledge with its help."

On hearing Modiji's demand Kanchan spoke out, "Sir, really one day you will change both the condition and the direction of India."

The words of Kanchan Banerjee are proved true. Today, after becoming the Prime Minister of India, Modiji is leading the country to a new prospect of development.

❑

Mudra Yojana

"Ramesh Babu, Ramesh Babu! What has happened to you? Buses are passing by you and where are you lost?" Deepak asked shaking Ramesh. Ramesh in distress turned back and saw his friend Deepak. Deepak took Ramesh out of the middle of the road by holding his hand.Both went to a park and sat down.

"Ramesh, what is the matter, brother? Today, you are looking very depressed."

"Friend, when there is darkness all around life, a man is left with no choice but to commit suicide."

"You are totally wrong, Ramesh. A courageous man braves challenges. Remember, there is no darkness in the world which cannot be turned into light. Darkness is to be removed. When the illumination of light spreads all around, there is no trace of darkness. First you tell me what hardship befell you that you are talking so negatively?"

"Deepak, you know I have been making bangles for years. To run my business well, I borrowed rupees thirty thousand at 10 percent compound interest from a local money lender in 2011. Since then I have paid 1.5 lakh in interest to the money lender but the capital amount is still intact. In this way I will be paying him for the whole life whatever I earn.

I do not know what to do."

Having heard everything Deepak said, "That's all. It is a very simple matter. You have borrowed from a wrong person. Anyway, no problem. Your friend is with you. He will sort out all your problems. Have you not heard about Prime Minister's 'Mudra Yojana'? Had you known about 'Mudra Yojana', you would have improved your condition very much by taking loan from it."

"No friend, I don't know about it. You know, I am not so educated."

"It does not matter. I am telling you everything about 'Mudra Yojana', today. The Prime Minister Narendra Modi inaugurated Micro-Units Development and Refinance Agency Ltd on 8 April 2015. Under this scheme small business men and skilled persons like you are given loan of Rs. 50000/ to Rs.100000/ to encourage them. You know the Prime Minister launched this scheme because people living in villages and remote places are devoid of the benefit of formal banking system. That's why they do not have access to insurance, loan, credit and other financial means to start small business or to promote one. Like you they depend on moneylenders for debt. A moneylender lends at a high interest. Therefore, such unbearable situations often emerge as it has happened with you. You would have been lying under the debt of the moneylender for the whole life; and if by chance I had not come across you today, I don't know, what wouldyou have committed!"

On listening to Deepak, Ramesh said, "Yes friend, you informed me of a very good thing. Really the Prime Minister has launched a very good scheme for a small businessman like me. Take me to the bank, today itself."

Deepak took Ramesh to the bank wherehe narrated

to the bank officials the painful story of Ramesh. The officials explained to Ramesh everything about loan under 'Mudra Yojana' and completed some necessary paper work. Shortly after it, Ramesh easily got loan of Rs. 50000/ at low interest. After getting loan from bank under 'Mudra Yojana' Ramesh first of all paid the principal amount to the moneylender and the rest he invested in his business. In a short time, his business started running well and he became the brand Ambassador of 'Mudra Yojana' in his area. Today, Ramesh helps all businessmen and skilled persons by giving information about 'Mudra Yojana'.

❑

Account Transfer

"Hello...Hello....Papa, what happened? Are you listening to me, what I am saying? Your daughter-in-law and I want that you should now shift to Delhi from Sonipat. At this age, you should be with your son. Now, I won't let you live there alone. I am coming tomorrow to take you. O K, I am now calling it off. You must be ready, Pranam." Saying this Praveen put down the phone.

Roshan Lal was overjoyed to hear such words of his son in this age. Roshan Lal was 86 year old. His son was employed in Delhi. He had settled there after marriage. He repeatedly asked Roshan Lal to accompany him to Delhi, but every time he refused. This time his eyes turned moist to find in his son's voice the feeling of both right and love.

Next day, Praveen reached there. Roshan Lal was working on his accounts. Praveen asked, "What's the matter, papa? What accounts you are busy with?"

"O Beta, it's nothing. I will have to get my pension account transferred to Delhi. I was calculating the same."

"Everything will be done, papa. Leave it all to me."

Thereafter, Praveen brought Roshan Lal along with him to Delhi. At the same time he submitted an application to the bank for transfer of Roshan Lal's bank account to Delhi so that he does not have to make a round of Sonipat for pension. Consequently, Roshan Lal's pension was stopped there, but his bank account was not transferred to Delhi. Praveen was very much troubled over it. He made several rounds of the bank at Sonipat; but every time he got the same parroted answer that the file is missing somewhere. In this process a year passed off. Praveen was very much distressed to make repeated visits of the bank at Sonipat. He shared this problem with his friend Rajkumar who in turn said, "Friend, you were unnecessarily troubled for so long. You should have lodged a complaint with the P M's office. Any way, it does not matter. Lodge a complaint now." After this Rajkumar explained everything about it to Praveen.

Having learnt everything, Praveen lodged the complaint with the PM's office on 21 August, 2015. Grievance Cell in P M's office that looks into such complaints sent it to Dept of Finance on 24 August, 2015. Prompt action was taken there. On 1 September, 2015, pension arrear along with his pension amount was credited to his account that was transferred to Delhi. At this Roshan Lal said, "Really, every complaint is resolved in a trice in Modi's governance. I was not expecting that the problem would be solved so soon."

On hearing it Praveen said, "Papa, the Prime Minister Modiji has made every work very transparent. So problems of common men like us are being resolved easily and without corrupt practices."

Roshan Lal acceded to Praveen and said, "Beta, give away sweets to everyone in the family today on this happy occasion."

"Yes Papa, of course." Saying this Praveen left for his office; and Roshan Lal, being pleased, thanked the Prime Minister and began reading the newspaper.

❑

The Effect of Petition

Shashi's friend Santosh Kumar asked, "Shashi, what's the matter? Today, you are wearing a sad look. You seem to have been troubled for quite some time. After all, what is the matter?"

"Santosh, how can happiness be seen on the face of a young man of twenty-eight who is unemployed?

"Friend, why do you lose heart? All would be well. Have faith in your hard work. The fruit of patience and hard work is always sweet."

"Economic condition of my family is very miserable. I took examination of group 'D' (Assistant/Peon) in Railway in 2013. I got through the examination. But I was disqualified on health grounds during the final ratification. However, I know that there was rampant corruption in it. I did not have any such health problem. I am not suffering from any illness. It pains me to see that you cannot get a job even after toiling hard."

Santosh said, "Do you feel that injustice is done to you?"

"What feel? Injustice is meted out to me. But to whom should I complain? Who will listen to my petition?"

"You should send your petition to the Prime Minister's office. Nowadays, serious attention is being paid to the problems of common men in PMO. Prime Minister, Modiji is committed to the development of common men and lower class people. He believes that the country will develop only when the whole people of the country step forward. Therefore, if you think so, you will get justice."

The words of Santosh gave him some hope. His eyes glittered with the radiance of enthusiasm. After that he sent his petition enclosing all relevant documents to the PMO on December 10, 2015.

After about fifteen to twenty days he received a phone call from a Railway official and his appeal was heard. After hearing everything his file was looked into and the complaint was found true. Redressing his complaint, the appointment letter was handed over to him in January 2016. Shashi was overjoyed to see it. He immediately informed Santosh on phone. Having got the news, Santosh rushed to Shashi and said, "Have you seen? Didn't I say that you will get justice if you file a complaint with Prime Minister's office?"

At this Shashi gleefully said, "Yes friend! Really, you have brought me Diwali in January itself. Come on, I will treat you to sweets."

After that Shashi took along Santosh to a confectioner's.

❑

Bank Account

Devendra runs a tailoring shop by the road-side at village Nisai in Pharukhabad district of Uttar Pradesh. His tailored clothes were highly admired in the village. However, honest Devendra could barely meet his two ends. He was not educated. He led a hand to mouth life. He happened to get a few rupees lying here and there in the house itself for odd days. One day Nimmo paid Devendra one rupee for stitching her clothes and said, “Baba, you should deposit some money in a bank. In bad days or during illness one's savings come handy.”

Devendra smilingly said, “Nimmo Bitia (daughter), how can I, illiterate, old, helpless man go to bank? I don't know anything about banking. I don't know anything, how to open an account and all its rules.”

Nimmo said, “Baba, you don't need to worry about all these things. Prime Minister has launched 'Jan-Dhan Yojana'. This scheme was launched on August 28. 2014. The aim of this scheme is to provide banking facilities to all households and to open account of every family. Not only this, our Prime Minister Modiji sent an email message to all banks before launching this scheme stating that bank account in every family is a national priority. That's why it is the duty of all citizens to extend support to this programme of the Prime Minister Modiji. I will help you. You take time off tomorrow. On government's instruction IDBI bank officials have organised a camp in our area. In this camp all those people like you who do not have necessary documents to submit to the bank for opening an account are being helped to open their bank accounts."

At this, Devendra said, "Beta, you told me a very surprising thing. Is it really happening in a country like India?"

Nimmo said, "Exactly Baba, not only this, it is taking place for the first time in history that bank officials are approaching the poor and opening their accounts in the bank."

"If it is so, I will definitely go along with you to have my account opened."

Next day, Devendra went to the camp with Nimmo. Nimmo provided Devendra all necessary information. In a short while bank officials opened his saving account. Today Devendra deposits his savings in his savings account and has learnt banking transaction system. Whenever Nimmo comes to him for getting her clothes tailored, he definitely says that Bitia, 'Jan-Dhan' is really a gift of the government to the poor.

Nimmo replies smilingly, "Yes Baba, now you see, till yesterday you were calling yourself illiterate and boorish. Today you are transacting everything with the bank yourself."

At this Devendra replied with a smile, "Yes Bitia, you are right. 'Jan-Dhan Yojana' not only taught me how to deposit money in the bank but also taught me calculation." Saying this Devendra smiled and Nimmo, too, smiled.

❑

E -Mandi

"Ramgopal, what happened? This time you had a bumper paddy crop. Every ear was filled with grain. Then why are you sulking?"

"Ratan, what to say! The crop was good but I was duped by middleman." On seeing the paddy Ramgopal making foul face said, "What gain is of this good crop? Everyone had a good paddy crop this year. Many farmers are ready to sell off good paddy at low price. In this situation I could get only a trifle in profit."

"Yes friend, you are right. Many a time we had to suffer loss because of brokerage of the middlemen and the onus is laid on the government. But do you know that Ujjawal conducts a programme related to agriculture on radio. He has come to stay with me for a few days. I will introduce you to him in the evening."

"Yes brother, do introduce me."

On seeing a well-built young man in the evening, Ramgopal learnt that this is Ujjawal.

Coming to Ramgopal he touched his feet and said, "Ram, Ram (expression of salutation) uncle. How are you? My uncle was telling that this year you had bumper paddy crop. Now get ready to receive the rain of wealth. With this, the paddy crop will usher in Lakshmi in your houses."

"How Beta, Tell me."

"Yes uncle, I am telling you everything in detail. You might be getting information about the policies of the Prime Minister Modiji."

"Beta, I do not get much information. I spend most of the time in my fields."

"It does not matter much, uncle. Now I will tell you everything in such a way that you will yourself take off time to view or listen to the information/ news. Modiji launched e-mandi that is electronic agro mandi (market) on 125th birth anniversary of Dr Bhimrao Ambedkar on 14 April, 1016 in Delhi. With this twentyone agro mandis in eight states of the country will get connected online."

"Beta, I am illiterate; go about slowly." Ramgopal said.

"OK... OK...uncle. Online means these mandis will be connected with a network of computers. With this, the price of all produces at different agro mandis will be known from one place. Not only this, with its help a farmer like you can decide the price of his produce based on prices available at different mandis and can sell his produce in any other mandi at higher profit without any help of middleman."

"Well done Beta! Though I could not understand completely, I certainly got that Modiji has started e-mandi scheme that is beneficial for the farmers."

"Yes uncle. Not only this, by the end of 2018, five hundred and eighty-five mandis will go online." In the meantime the sixteen year old granddaughter of Ramgopal came there and said 'Namaste' to Ujjwal. Ujjwal asked, "In which class are you studying?"

"I am doing XI with Commerce."

"Splendid! It's very good Rama. Now you should

keep your grandpa updated with the new schemes of the government related to farming. This will benefit him in agriculture and he won't be duped by middlemen."

Yes Bhaia, certainly I will do. Grandpa, hereafter, I will be informing you the prices at e-mandis and we will sell our produce there only. This will help us save on our expenses. Today, bhaia reminded me of it. Henceforth, it is my responsibility to check prices at e-mandis and negotiate the sale. After all, I have to become a charted accountant in future."

"Well done Rama! Excellent! If every daughter of our village gets education and rises forward, every programme of Modiji will be successful and the country will be seen marching ahead on the path of development."

Saying this Ujjawal addressed Ramgopal, "Uncle, I was telling you that Lakshmi will come to you. See, in the form of Rama Lakshmi has come to you.

At this everyone began smiling. Rama also joined them and Lakshmi was cheering in the fields of farmers in the form of Rama.

❑

Example of Good Governance

Once Narendra Modiji was discussing with his Cabinet Ministers the development and problems of India. Some Ministers informed him of the problems and developments of their respective regions. A Minister said, "Sir, development is taking place in every field now. Digital India has educated the villagers also. Not only this, it has become easy to provide facilities to far flung villages." This is how every Minister was relating himself.

Narendra Modiji listened to the Ministers and congratulated them on their good initiatives. At that time Modiji received a message that recently an Indian young woman Ujma Ahmad was deported to India at the initiative of Minister for External Affairs, Mrs Sushama Swaraj. Ujmaa Ahmad is the lady who was forced to marry a Pakistani national at gun point. The news of the safe return of that lady to India sent a wave of happiness among the Ministers present there. At this news, the Prime Minister Narendra Modi said to them, "The Minister for External Affairs Mrs Sushama Swaraj and her Ministry have created an example of the effective use of social media for giving good governance, and for rendering help to men and Indians trapped in any corner of the world. I want the same to be replicated in the whole country."

A Minister said, "Sir, in your regime every ministry has shown promptness in action."

The Prime Minister responded, "Not only in my regime but the competence and ability of the Ministers has also accelerated the execution. Ministry for External Affairs is now liked with the poorest of the poor in the country. When an Indian trapped in distress in any part of the world appeals for rescue, the Minister responds within just fifteen minutes. Besides, she is always accessible to the victims for help. A leader should be like this so that a common man should not take him as a leader but as his friend and can share with him his problem and have this hope in heart that prompt action will be taken on his complaint. I want that not only the Ministry for External Affairs should be like this but every Ministry should also be like this where everyone's problem is heard and quickly addressed to. When the people's faith in democracy rises, there is no doubt that the development for all with cooperation of all (Sabka Saath, Sab ka Vikas) will be realised." The Ministers agreed to Modiji's thought and pledged that they will also work in their respective Ministries with honesty and diligence.

❑

Triple Talaq (Divorce)

Once Modiji was talking about different issues related to the country. In the meanwhile, somebody referred to him Zakiya Soman, the founder of Indian Muslim Women's Movement. Actually Zakiya Soman's organisation had sent to him a memorandum signed by fifty thousand Muslim women. The memorandum sought to declare triple talaq illegal. After going through the memorandum, Modiji instructed his staff to provide information about the women who are victims of triple talaq and who are facing hardship.

The case of Shahbano was placed before him. On going through the case he learnt that Shahbano was divorced by her husband in 1978. She reached the Supreme Court to claim for maintenance allowance from her husband in 1981. In the court the husband refused to pay her maintenance allowance on the plea that he was not liable to it. Thereafter, many such cases came before the Supreme Court. In February, 2016, Shayra Bano, a resident of Kashipur, Uttarakhand filed a writ petition in the Supreme Court seeking ban on triple talaq, polygamy and halala nikah. She was married to a property dealer of Allahabad in 2002. Rizwan, the husband of Shayara Bano had brutally tortured her. After that he sent her talaq through telegram. Similarly, Afarin Rahman was divorced by her husband by sending a divorce letter through speed post in 2016. She is fighting against it in high court. A similar case was of Gulsahn Parween from Uttar Pradesh. Her husband sent her a divorce letter on a ten rupee stamp paper. Thereafter she also filed a case in the Supreme Court.

The Prime Minister went through countless such cases; and with this he came to know that Muslim sisters are leading a very scared life being terrified by the atrocities of their husbands. Many of the women who had been given triple talaq orally were in a very miserable condition. They were helpless even to make their two ends meet. Their children were also in a pitiable condition.

Modiji deliberated upon it seriously and decided that it is high time the society should change itself and a historic decision should be taken so that women get the full opportunity in every field to realise their dreams with freedom. He thought that India is such a country where we have women like the queen of Kittur, Chennamma, the queen of Jhansi, Laxami Bai and Jhalkari Bai who know how to take the English to task on their own. Therefore, in this twentyfirst century the custom like triple talaq must be abolished and for this a provision should be made in the constitution that gives both equality and freedom to the Muslim women. Now the proceedings in this regard went forth in the Supreme Court. A constitution bench was formed consisting of five judges of different religions. All the five judges were highly qualified and upright. They were Justice J S Khehar, the Chief Justice (Sikh), Justice Kuriyan Joseph (Christian), Justice Rohitan Phali Nariman (Parsi), Justice Abdul Nazir (Muslim) and Justice Uday Umesh Lalit (Hindu). Finally the historic day came when the Supreme Court, keeping in mind the profoundness of the constitution and the condition of the women in the country, declared 'triple talaq' null and void on 22nd August, 2017. With this India became the 22nd country in the world to ban 'triple talaq' and it was appreciated the world over.

This judgement sent a current of happiness among the women of the world. On receiving this news Jahida Heena, a noted Pakistani writer said, "I salute the Supreme Court of India for giving such a big judgement against 'triple talaq' and for the women's right. People may question why I should speak for the rights of Indian women or on a judgement there. But a woman is a woman, whether she is from India or Pakistan or from any other country. The voice of women should become the voice of the whole society and of the whole world. Then only the half of the population of the world in freedom and equality will be vocal and create history in the field of development and make a new road with freedom where the whole world will respect women, and progress in the interest of the countries."

Modiji welcomed this decision and said, "The judgement of the Supreme Court is historic. It is a milestone in the direction of women empowerment and in giving the right to equality to Muslim women." Thereafter, Modiji moved forward with firm footing and strong will power in a new direction to execute many decisive tasks.

❑

The Death of Fear

One day Prime Minister Narendra Modiji was sitting among the youths. The young men were sharing their curiosities and seeking his solutions. A young man said, "Sir, I suffer from examination phobia. I want to reach the zenith of success but I don't know how examination phobia pushes me back. As such, I do not get the result that I should get."

Many of them echoed the same fact. Everyone was scared of examinations, interviews and of undertaking new enterprises. At this Modiji smiled and said, "The youths of my country! What's the reason of your being scared of?"

A girl said, "Sir, the fear of committing a mistake is something we are most afraid of."

At this Modiji said, "Albert Howard has said a very important thing. All of you must know that. He said, 'The gravest blunder that a man can do is to be afraid of committing a mistake.' Do you want to kill this fear psychosis?"

All youths said, "Yes sir, we all want to kill this fear in ourselves."

Modiji replied, "When all of you are ready to end this fear in you; take it for granted that success is not far away from you. The best method to get released from the prison of fear is to keep yourself engaged in work. For example, some of you might be afraid of speaking from a stage. In such a case you must immediately practise speaking from a podium without thinking that you will commit mistakes. In doing so you will find that the fear is gone." Then he asked those who are afraid of speaking from a podium to raise their hands.

Many of them raised their hands. He called forward one of them and handing over a mike said, "Beta, speak about this programme today. Speak anything, but do speak." the young man got very scared to find himself standing before Prime Minister Modiji and the crowd of youths. Modiji said showing confidence in him, "I hope, you will be able to speak."

The youths also encouraged him.

Mustering his courage the young man took the mike closer to himself and said, "Today in this programme, I got the opportunity to speak something before Hon'ble Prime Minister Narendra Modi. It is a matter of great honour for me. This day will be unforgettable for me." After saying this, suddenly he could not believe himself that he spoke three-four sentences before the Prime Minister and the full crowd of audience.

With the applause of clapping the fear in him as in many other youths had died.

❑

Building New India

Narendra Modiji was warmly greeted in a felicitation ceremony. His actions were widely appreciated. In the public meeting someone said, "Since when you have talked about 'Sabka Sath, Sabka Vikas' (with cooperation of all, development for all) and continued with it as a credo; you have infused in us a different courage and self-confidence. Now along with completing our education, we want to make ourselves so competent that we can contribute to nation building."

Modi smiled approvingly to hear his words.

At that moment a girl student said, "Sir, since when you have opened all sectors for the women, the desire of every father is motivating his daughters to reach the sky. All this is made possible because of your work capacity and motivation." Many young men and ladies shared their thoughts and problems with the Prime Minister.

After listening to them Modiji said, "In democracy the government is formed by the majority but is run by consensus. The government is for all; it is meant to take along all. Alone, I am not the government. All my Indians are indispensable part of this government. Now I am seeing the dream of building a new India in the eyes of 135 crore

Indians. Now rising above politics, by 2022, that is on the 75th Independence Day celebration we have to build a new India in which everyone is entitled to education, home and basic amenities. I observe that in this public meeting most of you are youth and it is the country of dreams of youths, 65% of the Indian population. This new India is the India of the dreams of unprecedentedly conscious women. Now we all have to stand together while building this new India. The women of our country have made us realise by dint of their physical and intellectual ability that they can even grab the moon in their fists if they are given the opportunity. Now, I have to provide the same opportunity to every woman and youth of the country where they can hold the moon in their fists, prove themselves as founders and make a milestone in rebuilding this country."

At these words of Modiji the youths present in the assembly gave a huge applause that ushered the country on to the path of rebuilding with Modi's chariot of development soaring in the sky.

❑

The Profit of Peasants

On March 06, 2017 the Prime Minister reached Khushipur. A rally was organised there. A large number of farmers were assembled there. The farmers got enthused to see Modiji. An old and illiterate farmer told Modiji, "Saheb, we want that the productivity of the agricultural land should increase. We are most worried about the fact that if the productivity of the land does not go up, our income will not grow and poor income will adversely affect our livelihood."

On hearing the old peasant, Modiji said, "Bhai, I totally agree with you. I know that when we struggle and toil hard and do not get the return in proportion to the input, we feel very much disappointed. You should not worry about anything. To increase the productivity of land soil's health is being improved; the soils of the farmers' land are being examined. When the test report comes out, the farmers will be told to use the right fertilisers for higher yields. I do want myself that you should get the right price for your crops."

On hearing this many of the farmers' faces glowed. At that moment a female farmer stood up. She was young. She said, "Sir, I felt pleased to see that you are paying attention to the farmers. Only soil testing will not increase productivity. We have irrigation problem also. There is no proper irrigation facility here. You must take some step to address this problem."

Modiji was pleased to listen to the female farmer and said, "Sister, I am very happy that you put forward your opinion and problem confidently. I want that every sister of our country should be self-reliant and full of self-confidence like you. I am fully aware of the problem of water and irrigation. For this, we are planning to replace the old pumps free of cost. At the same time for the drainage of water drains are being constructed. We are also making programmes for water conservation. When these jobs are completed, your income will definitely go up. I am committed to double the income of farmers by 2022."

The peasants responded to it with great applause. On the face of every peasant there was a glow of happiness.

❑

Homes for the Poor: Development for All

The Prime Minister Narendra Modi launched the scheme 'Prime Minister Awas Yojana' on 25th June 2015. After taking over the responsibility of the Prime Minister in 2014 Modiji resolved to bring development to every nook and corner of the country and to the poor. When a meeting was going on in this regard Modiji said, "Financial aid should be provided to the homeless and to the incumbents of the dilapidated houses for construction of concrete homes under 'Prime Minister Awas Yojana'. This scheme should be implemented differently in villages and cities."

A leader in the meeting said, "It is an irony that even after 70 years of independence, around five crore families are forced to live without a roof over their heads. They are in dire need of homes." Another leader added, "You are exactly right. Since they are homeless, they are condemned to lead a miserable life in stinking slums. I have seen many old men selling candle sticks and balloons by the roadside. When a man has a home, his life style improves on its own; and when he is deprived of a home he does not shy away even from begging. To curb on begging, everyone particularly the poor must be provided with houses."

On hearing them Modiji said, “I agree with you all. Once a common man gets a house, his dreams come to life and his development takes place quickly.”

Then a local leader said, “If the poorest of the poor family has his own house, that family will rapidly move ahead on the path of development. Because having one’s own house is the extension of economic wealth; and at the same time it brings positive impact on education and health, and improves living standard.”

The Prime Minister said, “If every Indian has his own house by the end of seventy fifth year of Independence that is by 2022, the chariot of development of the country will move ahead swiftly. We will provide wings to every poor person through 'Prime Minister Awas Yojana'. This programme is not an infrastructure, but a programme tc bring life to the dreams of the poorest of the poor person. When a man's dream get wings, he gets ready even to measure the whole sky. Now we have to provide houses to our 135 crore people so that every Indian can fully and meaningfully contribute to the development of the country.” Thereafter, execution of 'Prime Minister Awas Yojana' began at fast pace.

❑

Adopt Tourism, Not Terrorism

On 2nd April, 2017 people were assembled near Battalbaliyan and Chenaini-Nashari tunnels since morning. In a shortwhile Prime Minister Narendra Modiji was to reach there. Besides the local residents, the youths of Jammu & Kashmir were highly excited. And the happiness of the youths who made their valuable contribution to it and worked on the construction of Chenaini- Nashari tunnel knew no bound. The people were anxiously waiting for the arrival of the Prime Minister. Finally the waiting came to an end and the Prime Minister arrived there. He greeted everyone with a smile and then inaugurated the country's longest tunnel --Chenaini-Nashari tunnel on Jammu-Srinagar National highway. The huge crowd at Udhampur was anxious to listen to Modiji.

Modiji said, "Today, India has laid a milestone in the history of the world. Chenaini-Nashari is not only a tunnel, but a leap forward in the development of Jammu & Kashmir. The sweat of the youths of Jammu-Kashmir went into its making. The youths are there to lend a new identity, a new glory to the country with their young aims and strength. But it pains me to see that while on the one hand some young men are engaged in transforming the fate of Kashmir by cutting through the rocks; on the other some misguided youths are lost in pelting stones."

At this some youths were heard saying, "We will make the future of the country bright, educate the whole country and will bring heaven like Kashmir throughout India by joining hands with you."

On hearing this Modiji said, "This is what I want. You have two ways- one is of tourism and another of terrorism. The game of bloodshed is good for none. If the people of Kashmir had dedicated themselves to tourism for forty years, it would have been a global tourist destination."

Then a wailing sound of a woman came from the crowd, "Prime Minister, I lost my son here."

On hearing the painful cry of the woman, Modiji said, "If you have lost your son in Jammu & Kashmir, India has lost their son. Now it is time we should march forward in unison and show not only to the Kashmir on this side but also to the Kashmiri people beyond the border how to develop Kashmir. This tunnel is the fate line of the valley of Kashmir."

A young man responded to this, "Sir, this tunnel has made communication easy for the tourists coming here and for the people of Jammu-Kashmir as well. This tunnel will promote tourism in Jammu and we will be motivated to seek employment in tourism. This tunnel has given employment to many youths. We have to link every young man with employment, so that our youths should never be misled to terrorism."

The Prime Minister was very happy to listen to him and said, "Well done Beta! I want to see the same positive thought and energy in 125 crore Indians. We will take the country forward together and carve out a new identity of India in which non-violence, love, harmony along with growth in standard of education, tourism and employment will be clearly visible."

The whole public gave their consent to Modiji by raising their hands and in this way Modiji moved a step forward on the road to development.

❑

Future IAS

Ilisha said, "Aishani, you are looking very happy, today. What's the matter?"

"Ilisha, today the Prime Minister Modiji came to the 92nd Foundation Course session of the prestigious Lal Bahadur Shastri Academy of Administration. I am feeling very happy to hear his words. Today, I am feeling proud of my mother. You know, she has been telling me since my childhood that Beti, if you have to serve the country, the best way is to join the prestigious Civil Services. This message of the mother has become part of my life since childhood. This is the reason why I stood fourth in the very first attempt of IAS." Saying this Aishani got lost in the memories of her childhood.

She used to sleep till late hours during holidays. While her mother used to write books for the whole night. Aishani said to her several times, "Mamma, you work in the office for the whole day and then you look after domestic chores as well and then you write books, too, despite being tired. Don't you feel tired?"

At this Aishani's mother said while taking her in her arms, "Beta, I do not feel tired at all. Actually, the work that we do lovingly with our heart in it does not give us tiredness but pleasure and calm. For me writing is a means of bliss and peace."

Breaking the stream of her thoughts, "Aishani, you are fond of reading books, aren't you?"

Aishani replied with a smile, "Yes, Ilisha, I got this habit from my mother. Till now I used to talk to books. But the Prime Minister has said today that it is good to learn from books, but we must be conscious and vigilant about those people in our surrounding whom we have to serve."

"Yes Aishani, the Prime Minister has also appreciated the avid readers of books. He said that lessons from books save us from deviating into the wrong path."

"Yes Ilisha! The Prime Minister further added that we can become good officers in future only by being connected with our team and the people and by having good relations with them."

"When the Prime Minister of our country pays visits to the future officers and students like us and encourages us, our self-confidence and enthusiasm automatically gets awakened."

"Ilisha, we will assimilate the words of the Prime Minister Modiji in our work. By doing this we will be able to validate his words that if the civil servants make the dreams and aims of the country their own, all problems of the country will gradually come to an end. I have made this promise to myself that after becoming a Civil Servant I will sort out the problems of the people and I will contribute to the best of my capacity to eradicate corruption, poverty and illiteracy from the country. So that in years to come India can make a distinct identity of its own in the whole world."

On hearing Aishani, Ilisha smilingly said, "I will do the same."

On hearing their talks even the walls of Lal Bahadur Shastri Academy of Administration got enthused with life and were ready to warmly welcome the future officers of the country.

❑

Drug Addiction

"Mukul, you have taken drugs today, again. I don't like at all to talk to you when you come drug addicted." Saying this Neha got ready to leave.

"Neha, stop please. If even you give up my company, I will be even more addicted to drugs."

"Ooh, why don't you understand? Drug is not a solution to any problem, Mukul. Odds come at every step in life. Do you know, my father has lost his job? There is no economic source available to me for studies, right now. Does it mean I should start taking drugs? If I take to drugs, my family will come to the verge of death. I am the eldest daughter in the house. I have so many responsibilities to shoulder. I can't even think of doing such nonsense."

At this Mukul sat down leaning his head on his hand. His eyes got moist with tears. Neha was his very good friend. Mukul was good at studies. A few days back he had lost his hand in an accident. He felt his life was dark after losing his right hand.

"What can I do, Neha? The goal of my life was to become an excellent archer. How is it possible now?"

"Everything is possible, Mukul. Just you have to shift your attention from your amputated hand to the wide world.

Have you heard the name of KAROLY TAKACS?"

"Sorry, I haven't."

"OK, today I will tell you about him. He was a sergeant in the army of Hungary. He was the best pistol shooter at the age of twenty eight in 1938. Everybody knew that in the Olympic Games 1940 he would win the gold medal. But during military training a bomb exploded on his hand by accident. His right hand blew off in it. Now think, a man who was the best pistol shooter in the country and suddenly his right hand blew off. What should he do in such condition? According to you he should have committed suicide. But no, he did not accept defeat; and started practising with his left hand. He had intense desire to win Gold medal for his country. He continued practising with his left hand and ultimately in 1948 his dream was fulfilled. He bagged a Gold medal in pistol shooting for his country with his left hand."

Mukul kept on listening to Neha in surprise. He said, "You are right. I have drowned myself in drugs. While, not only I but everybody knows that drug is very injurious."

Neha said, "Our Prime Minister Modiji has great expectations from the youths like us. Recently while warning people to keep away from drugs, he said drugs bring with it three things and they are bad three 'D'--darkness, Destruction and Devastation. Drugs take us to a blind alley, put us on the threshold of destruction. They hold nothing but devastation. Not only this, but he also told the youths that while taking drugs, the youths might feel getting loose from problems. But have we ever thought where does the money spent on buying drugs go? Think over it. If that money goes to terrorists, they would be buying arms with that and making the innocent people their target and killing the soldiers of our country."

Today Neha was shaking off Mukul's heart and mind. Mukul said, "Neha, Modiji also says that drug-addiction is so dreadful a disease that breaks even the healthiest ones. He is also of the view that one who has no aim, no motive, no desire in life is vulnerable to drug-addiction. Today your words reminded me of my goal. I promise that I will never take drugs hereafter and will not fall a prey to drugs under any pressure of problems and difficulties."

At this, a smile flickered on Neha's face. She said, "Then the day is not far when you will win for the country the Gold medal in pistol shooting in the next Olympic; and we would be clapping in your honour."

Mukul began smiling at Neha's words. With the smile on his face, happiness, too, knocked at his gate.

❑

Udan Scheme

Rinki's brother Udbhav said, "Rinki,come, let us play business, business."

Rinki and Udbhav both began playing. Udbhav was fourteen and Rinki was twelve years old. Whenever Udbhav saw an aeroplane flying in the sky, he got lost in imagining that a day would come when he will also travel by air and his dream would come true. The elder brother of Rinki and Udbhav Pankaj was twenty-two years old. He was employed at an airport. His father died of illness last year. Taking into consideration Udbhav's desire to become a pilot, his parents wanted to make him a pilot. But a lower class person can only have desires. To fulfil it is beyond his means.

On 27 April, 2017 in the evening, Udbhav was telling Rinki, "You will see. I am having an intuition that very soon I travel by air and will bring lots of toys for you."

Rinki laughed at it while saying, "Bro, it does not cost to make a castle in the air. Keep making castles in the air."

While coming in Pankaj heard their talk. He said to Rinki, "Udbhav's intuition is going to be true. Our Prime Minister Sri Narendra Modiji has launched "Udan Yojana" today. Do you know what does it mean?"

"What?'

"It means, the common man can fly in the aircraft. This scheme was launched by Central Minister for Civil Aviation, Ashok Gajpati Raju on 21 October, 2016 at New Delhi and it is being flagged off today on 27 April, 2017."

On hearing it Udbhav said, "Bro, it's all right, but how will my dream of air travel be fulfilled by it?"

Pankaj replied with a smile, "O fool! The main aim of this scheme is to make available air ticket at low price so that one who wears slippers can also travel by air. Now a common man can book a ticket for just Rs. 2500/ and travel by air. A common man cannot fly just in dream but in reality a distance of five hundred kilometres for just two thousand five hundred rupees."

"Brother, I am getting your point but what will the government get out of it?"

At this Pankaj smilingly replied, "My little brother, you are still innocent. The government wants to enhance regional air connectivity with the 'Udan scheme'. The government aims at boosting connectivity among forty-five non-serving or under-serving airports with this scheme. It will boost the growth rate of the country. With this 'Udan Yojana' is the first such scheme in the world, with which an attempt is being made to strengthen air connectivity along with increasing job opportunities in the field of tourism."

"Well done bro, if it is so, we will go on a trip by air along with mother in this summer vacation. Summer vacation is shortly to commence."

In the meanwhile his mother Uma stepped into the house and said, "Where are you three brothers and sister planning to go in the vacation?"

Pankaj answered, "Maa, this time, I will take you and them to tour by flight."

At this Uma said while turning to them in amazement, “O son, now I will travel in aeroplane in my next birth.”

“No Maa, not in the next birth but in this June itself.”

After this, Pankaj explained 'Udan Yojana' to his mother in simple terms. Having got all information Rinki and Udbhav felt overjoyed and were lost in the dreams of air travel in the vacation.

❑

Aadhar and Mobile

"Ashima, let us go to watch 'Secret Superstar' tomorrow. It is a very good movie. It's a picture mainly for youngsters like us. Jayra Wasim has performed very well with Amir Khan in it."

"Shubham, tomorrow is Saturday; it is a holiday in the office. I will first of all go to Airtel office tomorrow."

"Why? What do you have to do there?"

"O friend, I have get my mobile linked with Aadhar. Every day, this or that work comes up and I miss to get my mobile linked with Aadhar. Have you got your mobile linked with Aadhar?"

"O friend, why are you so hurried about it? We will get it done. Don't waste the day tomorrow. Let's go for a movie."

"Arre, despite being educated, what are you talking about? You know, Modi government is bringing several schemes to promote youngsters like us; and your attention is fixed to movie."

Shubham is possessed by the ghost of the movie "Secret Superstar" at this time. He reacted irritatingly, "OK, tell me what will it come to, if I do not get my mobile linked with Aadhar?"

"What will happen?It will be very fine, Janab. You must

be thankful to Modi government that is coming up with many schemes and technologies to protect you from frauds. By linking Aadhar to every work, corruption can be checked. You know, the government has taken up this step so that criminals, frauds and terrorists do not get a new SIM in the name of a common man and commit a crime. So, it becomes our duty that we avail of the schemes and technologies brought in for us and being educated we inform others about them. Whenever a mobile phone is stolen, we are clogged with so many odd thoughts because some criminal minded people are bent upon this. Spend only five minutes at a mobile shop and get your mobile linked up with Aadhar. After getting our phones linked up with our Aadhars we can easily reach the theatre to watch the movie also."

Seeing sense in Ashima's talk Shubham said, "You have a solid point. OK, tomorrow we will first link our mobiles with our respective Aadhar numbers and the move to watch the movie."

"Yes hujur, you will find me ready." Ashima said it in such a style that Shubham could not help smiling.

❑

The Field of Commerce

"Well done Ishita, you have got very good marks in Commerce. Besides getting first class in graduation, you are a topper. Congratulations!" Prasann said.

Sanskar remarked, "However, friend, I have heard that girls are not good at Commerce. Ishita has proved it wrong. Above all, Ishita's economic condition is not good. Still her mind works even more intelligently than Chanakya in Commerce."

Addha replied, "Where is it written that girls are not good at commerce or one who is economically poor cannot succeed in the field of Commerce? Where is it written, tell me, tell ?"

"You are right, Addha. Now everyone in our group knows that John Paul Dejoria and Do Wan Chang were very poor." said Ishita.

"Yes, Ishita, John Paul used to sell newspaper. He started Shampoo on loan and today his products are in high demand. He earned huge wealth."

"Exactly. Similarly, Wan Chang did many odd jobs and braving poverty at every step opened a cloth- shop and today he is counted among the billionaires of the world."

Prasann and Sanskar responding to them said, "Both

of you are very intelligent. You are aware of the foreign billionaires."

Ishita laughingly said, "Why, should we not have been aware of it?"

"And even otherwise, when Modiji is bringing in several programmes for the betterment of women along with promotion of business, then it is a must for every youth to have not only sound general knowledge but also have good knowledge of different trades and technologies." Addha said.

"You are saying perfectly right. Perhaps it is the impact of Modiji 's programmes that this year in the World Bank ranking India jumped thirty steps to secure its position among the top 100 countries for the first time. It happened for the first time in the history of the world when a country made such a quantum jump." Prasann said.

"Yes, you are talking about 'the ease of doing business report' of the World Bank. It is a good news. And it is true. Now it has really become easy to do business in our country. Modiji, with various new schemes, has made it easy to do business even in villages." Ishita said.

"Yes, absolutely. Schemes like Start-up, Prime Minister Mudra Bank, Prime Minister Skill Development, Gram Uday se Bharat Uday (Rising village to rising India) and several other schemes have invigorated the world of trade and commerce. It's a very good thing." Sanskar added.

Ishita made her point, "You know, the Vice President of the World Bank of South Asia division has said that the report on reforms in India indicates that India is fully ready to draw business. And our country is giving a tough contest to the countries in priority for business. The process of starting a business has speeded up now."

"In fact, the World Bank ranking makes it clear that India

has gained from the initiatives ranging from Demonetisation to GST and our economy has made its mark in the world. This time India has left behind countries like Ghana, Uganda and Vietnam. There is no doubt in it that our country will register itself among the top twenty countries in the world if youths like us take up business honestly as their career."

On hearing the conversation of these four Lakshay came there and said, "O my God! You are talking of trade and business as if you are the representatives of business from four different countries. Come, lets to have some food, we are famished. After all, Ishita has topped. So today's treat will be from her."

At this Ishita replied, "Certainly, I will give. Let's go, we will chalk out some business plan while having the party."

After that, all the five went to the canteen. The confident steps of these youngsters were pointing that India will become a big centre of business and develop speedily in the years to come.

❑

International Food: Khichdi

"Pranshi, let's go to canteen.I'm so hungry". Fatty Upma said dragging her.

"Just wait. Let me first complete my experiment. It'll go incomplete."

"Studious number one, you can also do your experiment after eating. Now move on."

Catching hold of Pranshi's hand Upma proceeded towards the canteen. On the way they met Chirag, Utkal and Triveni. Seeing them Upma cheeringly said, "Wah, what a pleasure we hardly meet because of our studies. Well, let it be in the canteen." Then they all headed for the canteen.

Pranshi and Upma were in the second year Chemistry Hons. Triveni was doing Hons in Mathematics and Chirag was doing Hons in Physics. Utpal was doing B.Sc. in Home Science. Most often they were pulling legs of Utkal that in future he would become either a chef or a lecturer in cooking.

As soon as they sat Upma said, "Today I am too hungry. I must have pizza, burger and chhole bhature."

How much can you eat, yaar! Break your eating speed and quantity of food. Utkal remarked."

"O man, why are you always after Upma?" Pranshi quipped.

"Now, let us place orders."

When they reached the canteen counter it was known that a quest team was going to visit the college. So today there was special Khichdi after their choice. Hearing it Upma was stunned. She blurted out "O my God! What to eat now?"

Pranshi spoke, "Have patience Upma, let'shave Khichdi today. However, for some time our country has made Khichdi not just international food, but it has also demonstrated its use and utility."

"Exactly Pranshi. On 4 November 2017 on the World Food Day world record of our native Khichdi was established at India Gate in Delhi." Chirag said.

"You all must have known that this Khichdi was prepared by our favourite chef Sanjeev Kapur along with ten experts." Utkal said.

"Yaar ! Why are you so effusive about Khichdi?"

"Upma, you too, should be equally effusive about Khichdi. Our Prime Minister Narendra Modi has played an important role in making Khichdi an international food item. We have seen that he does everything in a strictly planned way. In fact,Khichdi is such an item which can be cooked anytime, anywhere and anybody can make it. At least for me it is a very useful thing because I don't know cooking."

"Arre, it doesn't matter if you don't know cooking. We have already our Utkal to cook a variety of dainty dishes for us."

"Yes, I love cooking. I admit it and this time I watched very closely the recipe of 918 KgKhichdiwhich was prepared for world record. It was made from 125 kg rice, 45 kg moong dal, 3 kg bajra, 5 kg amarat, 2.6 kg jowar, 4 kg ragi, 10 kg ghee and beans."

Seeing it very surprised Chirag said looking at him, "Yaar, you are describing as if you were present at the time of making Khichdi."

"Arre yaar, one who seeks information, he has it from anywhere. Do you know why Modiji is publicizing Khichdi as brand idea or super food?

"No, tell us." said Upma.

"For you people so that fat persons like you may bid bye bye to fat and fast food. Do you know Upma, super food is one that contains omega-3 fatty acid, plenty of protein and fibre along with anti-oxidants, vitamins and other minerals. At present we in India generally eat fatty food. That's why several people in our country are suffering from cholesterol and obesity."

"Are you pointing to me?" Upma said.

"No, not just to you, rather to all fat persons like you. In our country most deaths account for faulty food habits. Therefore, if we eat Khichdi once or twice in a week it will maintain our good health and well-being. Did you follow fatty? So, you must include Khichdi in your diet. Modiji is doing a good work as he is committed to lead the country to a height of cleanliness and health."

"All right yaar! What you say is true. Let's eat Khichdi now." Then all ate Khichdi together.

Upma said, "Wah, on a hungry stomach Khichdi tasted very good. Henceforth I will regularly, practise exercise and minimize fatty and fast food to control my obesity."

❑

An Able Administrator

"Congratulations! A girl has been born".

Hearing it the father Dhruvjyoti Kalita was overjoyed. But in a few moments the doctor holding the baby looked rather worried. Seeing it Dhruvjyoti immediately approached the doctor and asked, "What happened doctor Saheb, is everything okay?"

The doctor looked worried. He said, "Mr. Kalita, you should keep patience at the moment. Courage and patience does everything all right. Also, have faith in God."

"Arre, will you people say something or go on placing a puzzle." Dhruvjyoti was getting restive to understand the doctor's words instantly.

"Nothing in particular. In fact the baby has some problem with its lungs. For this she will have to be shifted to a big hospital right now. If it is treated in time everything will be all right."

On hearing it all the joy of Dhruvjyoti was over in a moment. Holding his hand on his head he sat down. The doctor understood the condition of a father in such moments.

The nurse had the baby in her lap. She said, "Don't lose heart like this. My heart says nothing unpleasant will happen to the baby. But you must hasten your effort for her treatment."

Hearing the words of nurse Dhruvjyoti got up immediately and told the doctor, "Tell me, what to do?"

Promptly the doctor glanced at the list of the best hospitals in the country. Then without wasting any time he said, "Yes, Ganga Ram Hospital in Delhi will be the best for this treatment. Make arrangements to take the baby there."

Just after hearing the doctor Dhruvjyoti started making preparations to take the baby to Delhi. A baby of just 8 days was airlifted to Delhi. The baby and the escort party had to reach Delhi airport at 7 o'clock. This message was somehow conveyed to Prime Minister Modiji. The Prime Minister took prompt action just after getting the message. Now as Dhruvjyoti with the escort party landed at the airport with the baby, they were taken aback to see that the Delhi Traffic Police with Green Corridor was awaiting them. Along with Dhruvjyoti the escort party was pleasantly surprised to see it. Green Corridor took the baby and immediately made for the hospital. In just thirteen minutes the escort party carried the baby to the hospital.

Then and there a doctor's team took away the baby for examination. At a glance the doctor said, "Had there been some more delay, it would have been difficult to save the baby". Thereafter the baby was treated and because of timely treatment made available to the baby, she was successfully treated.

Seeing it tears welled up in the eyes of Dhruvjyoti. He said, "Today the life of my baby could be saved only because of the Prime Minister Modiji. The responsibility of the whole nation rests on his shoulders. In such a situation he felt the suffering of a father in his own heart. I will remain grateful to him throughout my life. Modiji provided all possible facilities for the child in a moment. Only an able administrator can do such a thing."

All agreed with Dhruvjyoti. In this way an able administrator like Modiji saved the valuable life of the child and gave a new life to the parents as well.

❑

India Rising from Village Rising

"Papa, I don't feel well in the village. I want to be educated. In my village the school is far off. I have a desire to acquire education. Please send me to my uncle in Delhi." Kamla told her father Babulal making an earnest appeal.

Babulal was absorbed in thinking. This year his wheat crop had been spoiled because of excessive rainfall. It was difficult for him to earn his bread. He himself had started thinking that now life was very troublesome in the village. Those were the things of the past when people used to say that there was life in the village. The fresh air in the village refreshes the mind and the body.

Seeing her father brooding, the twelve year old Kamla said, "What happened, papa? Why are you so silent?"

Hearing the repeated queries of Kamla Babulal emerged out of his reverie and said. "My child, next week your uncle is coming here from Delhi. I will talk to him to take you to Delhi with him and get you admitted to a good school there. I myself wish that you should study well and earn a good name for the country.

Next week both Kamla and Babulal were very happy. Since morning Kamla was overjoyed that her uncle was coming. Her uncle Chamanlal lived in Delhi. He was a Havildar. When he came embracing him Kamla said, "Uncle, what have you brought for me?"

Chamanlal knew that Kamla was interested in studies. He had brought for her colourful books of stories. Kamla treated her uncle to tea and breakfast. Thereafter the talks began. Seeing the condition of Babulal's home Chamanlal understood that the crops had failed and they were living from hand to mouth.

Chamanlal said, "Brother, you are not a conscious citizen at all. You have no idea of "India rising from village rising."

"No, I have no idea at all. What's this?"

"Arre, this is a very effective plan initiated by our Prime Minister Modiji. Under this plan the government is making all possible efforts to provide facilities and comforts in the underdeveloped villages. This plan was started on 14thApril 2016 from Mahu. This compaign is meant to promote social harmony in villages, to improve rural development, and to accelerate farmers' livelihood and their welfare who are the real protectors of the poor. This campaign is being run together with the state agriculture, labour, rural development, social justice and information and publicity ministries of the states. Besides this, this campaign is centered on village development, farmers' income, social harmony and welfare of scheduled castes and scheduled tribes. The other government plans already existing like Crop Insurance Plan, Health Card Plan, Deendayal Antyodaya Plan are also combined in it. These plans are for each and every village and citizen. Through the medium of these plans not only the means of livelihood will become easy, but the farmers' losses will also be reduced. Have you not availed yourself of any of these plans so far?"

"Arre, Chamanlal, when I have no knowledge of these plans, how can I take benefit of them?"

"Yes, what you are saying is true. It doesn't matter. I am here for ten days. In these ten days I will get all your work done. I will insure your crops, will get you Health Card and will also familiarize you with some other plans. So far as Kamla is concerned, she is very promising. I will get her admitted to a school in Delhi this year itself. When she is educated, you will feel proud of her.

Hearing it Kamla was beside herself with joy. Babulal also started discussing with Chamanlal the plans floated by Prime Minister Modiji to benefit from them.

❑

Price of Coronary Stent

"Ah! since morning I have acute pain in the chest," 67 year old Ranveer Singh putting his hand on the chest said.

"Papa, let's go to hospital just now", Govind said.

Then he took the necessary things and made for hospital with his father. Having examined Ranveer at the hospital they asked him to take certain tests. Govind was on the move for his father's tests.

After the reports came the doctor said, "Govind, your father's arteries are blocked. To open and remove them a coronary stent will have to be inserted. The sooner you get it done, it will be better for your father. If you delay, it may be the cause for your father's heart attack and most of the deaths in our country occur because of heart attack."

Hearing it Govind became afraid and began to think. He had heard from his friends that in need the heart patients are often given stent which is very expensive. He sat down holding his head with both hands. Govind was a clerk in a private company. How could he manage a very expensive stent for his father? He was deeply worried.

At the hospital all were attending to their patients. Suddenly a man looked at Govind thinking pensively. Seeing him he came to him happily and placed his hand on his shoulder. When Govind looked back, for a moment he forgot about his father's illness and said, “Krishna, You, here, how come?”

Krishna said, “One of my relatives is ill. I have come to see him. But I had no idea that you would be here. What brought you here?”

Govind started talking about his father. Krishna said, “Yaar, Let's go to canteen. We'll talk over there.”

At the canteen they ordered for food and started talking. For some time they talked about their olden days spent together. Then Govind said sadly, “Papa is a heart patient. The doctor says that arteries are blocked, and immediately stent will have to be inserted.”

“Then get it inserted, why think so much about it?”

“Arre yaar, you know my total salary is only twenty thousand rupees. How can I manage that heavy cost of the stent?”

“Who told you that you will have to spend a fortune for stent? Arre yaar(friend), ever since Modi government has come to power, it is making welfare plans for the common man every other day. Thus, the price of coronary stent to be used for the heart patient has been reduced by 85% by the government. Now different types of stent are easily available in the range of seven thousand to thirty one thousand. There was a time when a coronary stent cost from forty-five thousand to 1.21 lacs. Now the government has fixed its price.”

“Wah, you have told me a very good thing. But yaar, why has the government done it?”

“Because in July 2016 coronary stent has been listed in the National list of Essential Medicines. As per rules of NLEM whichever drug or device is included in this list, its price is determined by PNA. Till now, the metal made from which the common coronary stent was made was very expensive but now the same will be available at the price fixed by NLEM. From this step taken by the government lakhs of patients every year will have a benefit of 4450 crore a year."

"Krishna, by giving such information you have lessened my burden. In fact, this government is doing very good work for the common people. Now I can save my papa's life by buying a stent for him."

"Yes, Govind, now you should easily buy a stent and save your papa's valuable life."

Just then the waiter came with the food articles. Both of them began to eat and make plans of a happy future.

❑

Atal Pension Plan

"Bishnu, where had you been? You were not seen for two to three days." the vegetable vendor Dinu asked

"Leather had run short. Day before yesterday I had gone to buy the thing and yesterday I was indisposed, hence I could not come. Today your bhabhi was restless since morning. There was nothing at home to eat. Now, what to do Dinu? I don't have any permanent job on salary to get the money even when you are sick. Here I have to dig my well every day and drink from it."

"Yes, what you are saying is true. It is the same also with me. Sometimes I think that had I got some education in early days, I would not have faced such days. On many occasions it is not possible to have just two simple meals. In such a situation what to think of old age?"

While they were talking such things a young girl was seen coming towards them. Her sandals had broken. She told Bishnu, "Brother, these are my new sandals. I don't know how they got broken. Repair them carefully."

Bishnutook the sandals and began to repair them. Dinu was still standing nearby. He told Bishnu, "Lets us do together something so that we may spend our old age comfortably otherwise our life will become very troublesome. In old age our children do not have affection for us, not to talk of others."

"Yes, you are perfectly true. These days even shoes-sandal repair work is dull and listless."

The young girl was moved to hear their pain. She was an executive in an information company. Her name was Kavya. Kavya said, Are you people totally illiterate?"

Bishnu said, "I am totally a 'thumb man.' Somehow I can write my name."

Dinu said, "I have had classes up to V. I read the newspaper in Hindi."

Do both of you not know anything at all about Atal Pension Plan?

"No, what is this Atal Pension Plan?" Both asked startled.

"The NDA government of Narendra Modi started in 2015 'Atal Pension Plan' to give the benefit of pension to people like you. This plan is for a common man. If you join this plan you will not have to depend on others in old age. This plan is beneficial for poor people as well as middle class people. Those people whose income is not regular or have low income job, for them this plan is most effective."

"Good! Madam, tell us about it in detail."

"Listen to me attentively. People between 18 to 40 years of age can join this plan. If today your age is below 40 years then when your age becomes above 60 years you will start getting pension every month. In this way you will not depend on others in old age."

"My age is 31 years now" Bishnu said.

"And my age is 29 years."

"Well, then both of you can take advantage of this plan. For this both of you must have your Aadhar Card."

"Both of us have got our Aadhar Card," Dinu said.

"It is very good. Now, in order to take advantage of this plan you will go to a bank. Have both of you opened an account in a bank?"

"No, I don't have an account in a bank", Bishnu said.

"I have my account in a bank", Dinu replied.

"Don't worry. It is a must to have an account in a bank in order to join Atal Pension Plan. Your monthly premium of Atal Pension Plan is directly deposited from your account. Therefore, once you join this plan you will not have to go again and again to deposit your premium. No doubt, you will surely have to leave some balance in your account so that your premium may be regularly paid.

"Madam, you told us many useful things. Now please tell us at what rate are we supposed to receive pension?"

"In this plan there are five denominations of pension 1000, 2000, 3000, 4000 and 5000. You are to choose how much pension you want to have per month after your age is 60 years. Suppose, today your age is 18 years and after 60 years you want a monthly pension of rupees 1000, then you will have to deposit a monthly premium of Rs. 42. And if you choose to have a monthly pension of Rs. 5000, your monthly premium amount will increase, you will have to deposit Rs 210 per month. The bank will give you all the information in this connection."

"Wah, the premium amount is not much. The government has made a very good plan for poor people like us. Lo, Madamji, your sandals have been thoroughly repaired."

"How much to pay?"

"Arre, Madamji, now how can I accept any money from you? You have given us very good information to make our life easy."

"Arre, that's my duty."

Thereafter Kavya handed a note of Rs. 20 to Bishnu and went her way. Seeing her go away, Bishnu told Dinu, "Alas, if all people become helpful as Kavya, our country will become a heaven.

"Yes, you are right. Tomorrow both of us will go to bank with Aadhar cards. Now, let me sell my vegetables."

There after Dinu moved on with his loaded trolley calling buyers and Bishnu was engaged in his own work. Today both were happy as they had got information to make their hard work bear fruit and secure a sustainable future. ❑

Public Grievances Redressal

"Sir, I, Kasturi have come for 'Modi Plan' for the poor." The assistant of State Bank of Travancore was busy with his work. He did not listen to the words of Kasturi attentively and completing requisite formality opened an ordinary account in her name. Kasturi was illiterate, so she did not know that instead of Jan Dhan Account, she had been opened an ordinary account. Where she worked, the in-charge Rachit Shyam was a very polite person. He had advised Kasturi to get a Jan Dhan Account opened in her name. He realized that an ordinary account had been opened in the name of Kasturi. Rachit Shyam said, "You go to thebank again and go with the application duly filled in."

Finding time Kasthuri went to the bank and told the officers there, "I had asked to open a Jan Dhan Account but the bank people opened an ordinary account. I am very poor."

The words of Kasturi fell flat on the bank officer. He said, "Now this plan has been closed, so we can do nothing in this matter."

Kasturi told it to Rachit Shyam. He himself went to the bank and said that he had himself sent Kasturi to the bank to take advantage of that plan. She was illiterate but the staff should have inquired about her need. Even the bank officer paid no need to the words of Rachit Shyam and went on doing his work. Seeing it Kasturi told Rachit Shyam, "What will happen now?"

"Don't you worry, I'm here. Everything will be all right. Now let us go back."

After returning from the bank on 22 January 2016 Rachit complained on the Prime Minister's portal and gave a detailed account of Kasturi's story. Very soon after this, a miracle happened. Kasturi and Shyam Rachit were surprised to see that the very third day the bank officer himself telephoned Kasturi asking her to go to the bank immediately. Kasturi could not understand why the bank men had called her to visit the bank immediately. She replied simply, "I go to work in the morning itself. I can see you at seven in the evening."

The bank officer said. "If you find time please come to bank today at 7 o'clock."

Kasturi conveyed it to Rachit Shyam. He was also surprised. He said, "It appears that the complaint on portal has been very effective. You must go to the bank today itself."

When Kasturi reached bank at 7 o'clock, she was surprised to see that the bank officer was impatiently waiting for her.

The bank officer sought necessary information from Kasturi and then opened her Jan Dhan Account. Seeing it for the first time Kasturi realized the power of the poor person. Very happily having a Jan Dhan Account opened in her name she reached home. Next day she went to work and told Rachit Shyam about it. Rachit Shyam said, "Congratulations! At last your Jan Dhan Account was opened. It really is a sign of good administration and true empowerment."

Kasturi said, "Yes Saheb, this government has shown a new way for us and made life simple for people like me." Thereafter she applied herself to work happily. ❑

Education Loan Portal

"Sankalp, what are you thinking? You have topped in Science subjectsat your school. Now you are very close to your dream. You want to become a doctor, don't you? I hope you will also pass the Medical Entrance Test", Ambuj said.

"Yes my friend! I know that I will also pass the Medical Entrance Test, but the problem is how can I manage the education expenses? You know, my mother earns our livelihood by tailoring and weaving. There is only my mother at home. She provided me with education up to this level, but how can she afford the heavy expenses of Medical Education?

"Arre, why do you think such things? Every problem has a solution. However, I have a solution to this problem."

"All right, tell me, what's the solution?" Sankalp said.

Ambuj replied, "Despite being so talented how did you not remember that for promising and laborious students like you Modi government has launched a portal titled www.vidyalakshmi.co.in for education and loan. You should know that this portal has been created keeping in mind specially students like you. Many students have to give up their high dreams in the absence of a means to pay the fees but now it is not so. Because of this plan no student like you will have to compromise with his future.

"Arre, wah, Ambuj! It is true that sometimes one fails to notice certain important things. Really Modi government has made this very useful plan. I know all about it. Its procedure is also very simple. Under this plan one has just to fill in a form. In this plan 13 banks have registered Education Loan Scheme in this portal. It includes SBI, IDBI, Bank of India and Canara Bank. This portal is being developed and controlled by NSDL e-governance infrastructure. Yaar, just fish out your mobile. Let's search this scheme." Sankalp said.

Instantly Ambuj opened on Google www.vidyalakshmi.co.in and there appeared 'Vidyalaxmi' portal in capital letters. After log in Sankalp filled in his mail ID and had a glance at the loan option. There was also description of the loan interest.

"Now I go home and register myself on www.vidyalakshmi.co.in portal as well as deposit Id proof address online. From this I can avail myself of this scheme."

"Yes Sankalp. On this portal loan is also available for higher education besides vocational courses. Previously the people from poor families could achieve higher education by luck or by giving private tuition, but it is not so now. All options have been opened by Vidyalaxmi portal", said Ambuj.

"Yes Ambuj. From Vidyalaxmi portal every student of the country can get vocational education. Not only this, previously whereas because of expensive education the poor but meritorious students had to limit themselves upto graduation degree and then had to find employment, now it will not happen so. It will minimize unemployment and several promising students will be able to start their own business."

"Sankalp, what you are saying is true. Yaar, now I have found a solution to your problem. Now smile and get ready for celebration."

Hearing it Sankalp smiled and said, "All right. Let's celebrate it. Today I will treat you to ice cream.

Hearing of ice cream Ambuj was overjoyed and headed to have ice cream with Sankalp.

❑

Community Medicine Centre

"Khin... Khin..... Khin...... ah, I'm half dead coughing" old Saifuddin spoke coughing still sitting on bed.

His son Amin came to him running. He passed his hand around his waist and told his sister Najma, "Go and immediately bring water for Abba." Amin gave water to his father and then he felt relieved. When he composed himself Amin told Najma, "Today I have to attend an interview. If I get the job everything will be all right. You will look after Abba."

Najma said, "Yes brother. You attend your interview freely." Najma was also doing B.A. from a college. Her expenses were also met by Amin. He gave private tuition in mathematics to some boys. Recently he had done a course in Pharma. He was in search of a job, but was not able to clinch it.

After the interview Amin realized that even there he had no chance of getting a job. He went to friend Nilesh who was his good friend. Both of them exchanged their views as well as problems. Noticing marks of disappointment on the face of Amin, Nilesh understood that today also Amin had returned empty handed. Seeing Amin absorbed in thought he said, "Yaar, it will not do to sit sulking like this. We must find out a way. Just wait, let me have a look at the Prime Minister's schemes. These days Prime Minister is launching several plans for poor young men like us." Then he opened the Prime Minister's schemes.

Nilesh went through Prime Minister's Skill Development Plan to Prime Minister's Poor Schemes. Suddenly he caught sight of Prime Minister's Community Medicine Plan. He opened it and read out to Amin, "Prime Minister's Community Medicine Plan is a campaign set up by the Pharmaceutical department of the Government of India. Under this plan government will open more than a thousand community medicine centres in order to make available medicines to common people at 60 to 70% less price than the market price. And the happy thing is that already 100 percent community medicine centres have been opened by now. In these centres a commission of 16% is given on the sales of medicines. According to this scheme the government supplies generic medicines to these centres regularly."

Seeing him speaking continuously Amin spoke rather annoyed, "Stop Yaar, what's there for my interest that you are taxing my brain for so long?"

"Arre yaar, you are getting annoyed before hearing them how can I suggest you something? There is something of your interest."

"Yaar, tell me quickly. At home Najma will be alone looking after Abba"

All right, you go home. Just let me tell you that previously this plan was limited to the select institutions of the government, but now any pharmacist or doctor can open Community Medicine Centre. It will not cost much and you can take a loan from Prime Minister's Plan. Thus, whereas now you are looking for a job, people will come to you for jobs. I have full faith in your laboriousness. You must do your utmost to open a Community Medicine Centre. I am with you. It will also benefit your Abba. Costly medicines will be available to you at a small price."

"Wah, yaar! you have really told me something of my interest. A friend should be like you. You have suggested a fine pathfor me. Right now I will start getting the details about it." Saying it Amin moved on towards home with zeal and confidence after hugging Nilesh warmly.

❑

Amrit Mission Plan

"Raju's papa, because of rains there is mud all around. Water has entered the rooms. The roof is leaking. Children are crying because of hunger. Is this life! I don't know why you insist that you will not go elsewhere selling this house. Arre, you will never earn enough to buy any other house. Then what is the harm in selling this house and buying another. I say let us go to Delhi. Delhi is not far off from Shamli. There I will find some work of my choice. My sister Sumita lives there. She says that most people in Delhi have a maid to sweep and wipe the house and do other domestic chores. They also pay handsomely. That will also be a help to you."

Ramesh was in a deep dilemma. Hearing the nagging from Saroj he said, "No more of it. You talk a lot and that too without thinking. You say let's go to Delhi and sell this house. Have you ever thought where you will live in Delhi? The place is so expensive and there is so acute congestion that in a single flat ten people have to live somehow. Here we have a house of at least 60 to 70 metre in which we are living. No work is a child's play. For every work one has to plan and think, understand! We can also improve living in Shamli."

Just then Raju came holding his books. He was a student of class nine and a very intelligent one. Noticing the parents arguing he said, “Ma and papa, both of you are arguing uselessly.” Then looking towards ma he said, “Because you have no knowledge of Amrit Mission Plan launched by the Prime Minister, therefore you are asking papa to go to Delhi.”

Hearing it Ramesh said, “My son, what’s this? Even I don't know about it. Tell me in detail.”

“Papa, you already know that our Prime Minister is launching several new plans for the common people and is trying in every possible way to improve their standard of living so that there may be everybody’s development in the country.”

“Yes my boy, that I know but I don't know about Amrit Mission”

“It doesn't matter, let me tell you.'Amrit Mission' is such a plan the purpose of which is to make available the basic facilities like water supply , sewerage, city transport etc. The aim of this plan is to improve the quality of people's life, particularly of poor people like us and the differently-abled people.”

“My Son, why is this plan called. ‘Amrit Mission’?”

“Papa, the full name of this plan is ‘Atal Mission for Rejuvenation and Urban Transformation i.e. Amrit.”

“But my son, what are we to gain from it?”

“Ma, you have asked a very good and useful question. This plan will benefit us because our Shamli has been selected for this plan. Where this mission will be made effective, there a few villages and localities have been selected. Under the plan in the selected places proper supply of water, improving sewage facility, cleaning septic tanks and night soil, drainage for flood water and city transport will be streamlined. Under this plan the government will make arrangement for supply of water in remote areas, the water supply system will be created and maintained, underground sewage system will be created and maintained as well as lanes and septic tanks will be mechanically and biologically cleaned. Work on these plans is going on. When the government is bringing in such beneficial and useful plans for us, it is also our duty to co-operate with the government. You will soon see after sometime the problems we are facing today will no more exist. In the near future our Shamli will become a clean and fine locality. But we toowill have to take a step further for improvement and cleanliness."

Hearing it Saroj said with a smile, "Yes my son, from Amrit Mission it appears that all our troubles will come to an end. I get upset at trifles. I will not repeat them."

At the words of Saroj both Raju and Ramesh were smiling.

❑

Namami Gange Plan

"Fie, Fie, they don't care about dirtying. See, they must have come to have a dip in the Ganga, one of them has thrown away this corn cob. In the morning come to have a bath in the Ganga and seeing the filth the mind feels nauseated," Pandit Ramnarayan said prattling.

Pandit Deendayal Chaturvedi was standing nearby. He said, "Panditji, it is no use blaming others. Whether it is the cleanliness of the Ganga or any place, it cannot be cleaned until and unless all of us co-operative with our word and deed. The government has done a very good thing while starting Namami Gange Plan. This is the dream mission of our Prime Minister Narendra Modi. We all know that due to release of untreated sewage and industrial waste into the Ganga in a large quantity for years together, its condition is worsening day by day."

By then other Pandits had also turned up at the Ganga Ghat. They also joined this discussion. Pandit Govind Mishra said, "The government has taken a good decision to start Namami Gange project to make the country clean and decent. This project covers almost the whole country. This project is spread over the whole north India along with north-west Uttarakhand and West Bengal in the east."

Hearing it Deendayal Chaturvedi said, "Yes Mishraji, you are right. The five states of India Uttrakhand, Jharkhand, Uttar Pradesh, West Bengal and Bihar fall on the way to Ganga. At same time because of its tributaries it also touches Himachal Pradesh, Rajasthan, Haryana, Chhattisgarh and some parts of Delhi. Thus this project includes these areas, too.

Pandit Aniruddh Upadhyay said, "It is clear that from this project the tributary rivers and these areas will be cleaned. At present where this river passes through, the industrial units deposit their waste in it which pollutes the river. Now this position will be checked." Chaturvedi said, "The biggest problem of this river is its length. In addition to covering a range of 2500 KM it covers 29 big cities, 48 towns and 23 small towns."

Pandit Ramnarayan said, "Chaturvediji you can't help sharing your knowledge of the four Vedas. Now, where is the question of length or areas? But had you not told us these things how could we know that among us pandits you are the most knowledgeable as well as a writer." Hearing it Mishraji said, "It also applies to Ramnarayanji. It is Chaturvediji who solves our each and every problem and the most important thing which I have learnt from him is that he does not hesitate to pick up the waste lying anywhere and deposit it in the dustbin. This is really a big thing. We all keep our homes clean, pick up the waste and filth but hesitate to collect the waste from the path. In the situation just think, how will the Namami Gange project succeed? To make it a success all of us will have to come forward with a firm determination and try to clean the common sites."

"Quite so, you are right to say so Mishraji, Henceforth we will not hesitate to collect waste from the road," Ramnarayan said.

"Arre, will you just go on discussing. It is time for aarti. Let us go for Puja."

"It is my belief that if we have wholeheartedly resolved to clean the Ganga, this is true puja and aarti."

Hearing it all pandits said, "Jai Gange! This very moment all of us take a solemn resolve to maintain the Ganga clean."

Hearing these words the waves at Ganga Ghat leapt up. It seemed that hearing of the cleanliness Ganga had given her silent approval out of joy.

❑

Asian Summit 2017

"Anant, this time you must go to the agriculture fair with your new variety of carrot. There it will be really appreciated by the agriculture scientist." Pankul said.

Pankul and Anant were not only good friends, but also young farmers. Anant had done B.Sc. in agriculture and Pankul in Botany. Both of them lived in Hiranki, a village in Delhi. They had their education in Delhi, so they were wiseand knowledgeable farmers. Both were aware of the latest changes in agriculture. Anant used to read two newspapers every day. That day also after reading the newspaper. Anant told Pankaj, "Yaar, Modiji has carved out a distinct identity even in Asian Summit. There he not only earned a name for our country, rather a laboratory has also been named after him."

Hearing it Pankul said, "Yes, I had seen the news on TV about it but as I was engaged in domestic matters, so I could not check it closely. Why had Modiji gone to that laboratory?"

"On his Philippines tour in Asian Summit- 2017 Modiji went to World Rice Research Centre there. There he gave seeds of two varieties of rice to the gene bank of that centre and also used the spade. Look, here is the photo of Modiji in the newspaper showing him working with a spade. This very laboratory had been named after him and that is a big honour", Anant said to Pankul showing the newspaper.

Reading the news Pankul asked, "What is the function of this laboratory?"

"Arre yaar, being such a good and educated farmer you have no idea whereas rice is your favourite dish," Anant said with a smile. He told Pankul, "The International Paddy Research Institute by improving farming is playing an important role in alleviating poverty and starvation. The Indian scientists are making discoveries every day. Do you know that during his tour Prime Minister Modi talked to the Indian scientists at this institute located in Los Banos 65 km away from Manila. The scientists of IRRI told Modiji that now there are certain varieties of paddy that survive even in case of flood. What a big achievement! From such crops better yield can be achieved in flood affected areas and the most important thing is that rice fads like you will never face the shortage of rice as it had happened during Prime Minister Lal Bahadur Shastri."

"Anant, you are really a genius. You know everything. Really our Prime Minister is carving out a distinctive identity of India. I had seen a few episodes of Asian Summit 2017 on TV. There all the great leaders were in suit but our Prime Minister Modiji went to the stage on Indian kurta pajama and left an incredible stamp on all present there. Modiji is laying stress on saving and promoting civilization and culture of India at the same time encouraging to adopt the new and sophisticated techniques. That's why our country is transforming day by day."

"Yes, Pankul, at the Asian Summit 2017 Modiji also said that we have emphasized on "Act East policy" for the development of the country because we feel one with these countries. We Indians do not take from others, rather we give them and we never snatch at all. Don't you realize that from such matters Modiji enhances our prestige a hundred times. Hearing such things I am full of zeal and self-confidence and regard it as my duty to contribute my best leading the country in a new direction."

"Me too, yaar! Really Modiji has created love for our country in us young men and this love for the country one day will make our country the best in the world," Pankul said.

Just them Anant's mother Rukmini came with food for them and they stopped talking. Rukmini told Pankul, "My son, today I have cooked fine brand of rice for you. This rice is the outcome of Anant's sowing."

Pankul's nostrils started fluttering from the scent of rice and he then and there took on the food. Both Anant and Rukmini were smiling to see it.

❑

Prime Minister of the Country

"Arohi, this time you will win the President's election in the college. You are not only a good speaker but also your ideas are innovative. And our college needs such a President who is one with the students in solving the problems of students," Aradhya said

"Arre Arohi, flatterer stop. You are flattering her day and night", Sarthak said.

"No yaar, not just flattering. Aradhya was not wrong. Arohi is such a noble soul that she can attract anybody with her goodness and even startle one with her talent," Tejas added.

"Oh ho.... ho..... Saheb gets no chance to admire Arohi, so today you have got an excuse to open the tender feelings of your heart before Arohi," Sarthak said.

"Arre, stop talking yaar! You people have got on to pull each other's leg. We all know, Arohi is the best. Don't Arohi?" Tanya said.

"Now what can I say about it? I just believe in doing my work well."

Tejas said, "Arohi, if you go on advancing like this, I have no doubt one day you may become the second lady Prime Minister."

Sarthak said, "Stop yaar, it's too much. However, our Prime Minister Modiji is running the country very well. After all winning 282 seats in the Lok Sabha is not a small thing."

"Yes, you are perfectly true. I am myself very much impressed by the merits of Modiji. Do you people know that he is the first Prime Minister who as the missionary of his parent association Rashtriya Swayam Sevak Sangh visited 450 districts out of 688 districts of India. From his hard work he became an office bearer of the national unit of Bhartiya Janata Party and then the Chief Minister of Gujarat. Not only this, only a man of strong personality like Narendra Modiji could successfully carry out a difficult feat like surgical strike. After becoming the Prime Minister and realizing the suffering of the common people and their problems he has initiated several projects for them."

"Wah, you have comprehensive knowledge about Modiji. You are correct to say that the lower class people have benefitted from many of those schemes," Tanya said.

"Modiji has also taken home policies very seriously and reformed them. He has emphasized for promoting peace and harmony in the country that Aligarh Muslim University should not be regarded as "Minority University" as well as voicing total disagreement with "Triple Talaq" he has made all possible efforts to legislate a law in this regard," Arohi said.

"Our Prime Minister is known as 'development personality' i.e. Vikas Purus and he is the one Indian leader with the greatest number of followers on micro blogging site twitter. Time Magazinehas placed him among the powerful leaders of the word," Aaradhya said.

"Modiji embodies all merits in him. He is interested in both reading and writing. He has published books like

'Setubandh' Ankh aa Dhanya Chhe, Karmayoga and Jyotipunj. I have got his Karmayoga and Jyotipunj both", Tejas said.

"It seems to me that in the years to come our country will present a new picture in technology, education and industrialization," Tanya said

"Of course! At the moment it is time for Arohi to pursue his publicity work. Let us co-operate with Arohi whole heartedly in his Publicity campaign so that Arohi may win the President's election by a thumping majority," Sarthak said.

"Yes, you're right," Tejas.

Thereafter all of them engaged themselves in preparing for the election.

❑

Modi's Personality

"Shiv Yaar, every moment you are seen sweating in the gym. Yaar, find some time to spend with me," Rohit said.

Arre yaar, Shiv has no time for us. The brother is President of the college. He has lots of responsibilities of students of the college, added to it the gentleman has a passion for reading and writing. He takes only vegetarian diet. He is a teetotaller. He believes in honesty, work and Industry," Raj said.

"In a way friends, our Shiv is perfect marriage material," Samarth said.

"Enjoy making fun of me. Arre yaar, reading-writing, eating vegetarian food, taking exercise are part of my life's routine. I have been so since my childhood. There is nothing to speak of so highly," Shiv said.

"Yaar, surely it is a matter of admiration. After all, we are not like you," Rohit said.

"Well then, why should you be will like me? I like it is very much. Among us he is the most honest, gentle and simple. You will see one day he will certainly make his mark," Shiv said pointing to Raj.

Raj said, "I don't know whether I will make a mark

or not but I am very much impressed by the personality of Modiji. The secret of his success is his hard labour. Right from childhood till today he has achieved this seat by dint of hard labour. During election he slept only for 3 to 4 hours. After becoming Prime Minister he regularly works for 18 hours every day."

"Yes Raj, you are right to say so. Not only this, his voice is bold and he has a miraculous art of speaking. Wherever he goes, people become his fan. In Rajasthan he speaks of the specialties of Rajasthan and in Gujarat of the exclusiveness of Gujarat, likewise in Uttarakhand and Bihar he discusses their problems seriously. He also attracts people with his dress. That's why he has become a style icon in the whole world," Shiv said.

Now Samarth and Rohit also jumped into the fray to register their opinion. Rohit said, "Ever since Modiji has assumed power, he has been working regularly as an able CEO. So he has been frequently teaching his MPs and strictly instructing them to take part in the proceedings of Parliament and reach there on time. Not only this, if he is not satisfied with one's work, he does not hesitate to relieve him from the post and promote a suitable and deserving one in no time."

"I feel inspired by his sense of discipline. Very easily he performs four to five rallies in a day. He is equally punctual. Even at the age of 67 he appears totally fit and healthy. The responsibility of the whole country lies on his head and he meets it is very happily. He gets energy both physical and mental from Yoga. He does yoga regularly, eats simple food and self-confidence and zeal adds to his personality," Samrath said.

Endorsing the words of Samarth Raj said, "Narendra Modi has positive and optimistic outlook which enhances his being. He is not deterred by criticism and retorts criticism in the same coin. He thinks creatively and believes in working through creative projects and works."

"Raj, you are hundred percent true, not only this, he also listens to common man carefully. Every month in the radio programme 'Man Ki Baat' he speaks on matters related to people and on complaints and suggestions received. He is constantly moving forward to development taking everybody along. And the steps of India are on to reach the zenith. If we co-operate together with Narendra Modi, our country will not only move forward, rather all of us will move forward," Shiv said.

"Yarr, from today, let us try to awaken the illiterate people. Thus we will directly not only serve the country rather we can also satisfy our inner self," Raj said.

"Let's go, start this noble work from today itself. After college hours we will teach illiterate peoplefor some time so that they may also contribute themselves in nation building," Samarth said.

After that they moved on towards respective classes to go after classes are over to Jagdamba camp to awaken the people there.

❑❑❑